THE SNOW DAY MURDERS

AN EDWARD CRISP MYSTERY

PETER BOON

CONTENTS

*For the boys at Bowden House School - go forward
and achieve your dreams, remembering We Not Me.*

Map Of Chalk Gap Village

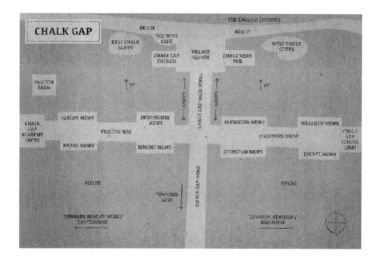

1

Everyone always remembers a snow day. Especially if you work or study in a school. Your normal, dull, grey routine is replaced by a magical winter wonderland, where everything is pristine white and anything is possible.

Noah, my student library assistant and now my foster brother, was certainly buying into that last one.

'What if we all get trapped in the village and a murder happens? Thick, deep snow as far as the eye can see. No one can go in or out so it must be one of the villagers. But who? The police can't even get into Chalk Gap, so hotshot amateur detective, Edward Crisp, and his trusty teenage sidekick, Noah Oxley, must solve the crimes themselves.'

'Not this again, Noah.' I didn't want to think about how last time Noah imagined us in a murder mystery, his prediction came eerily true.

There's so many classic murder mysteries where everyone is snowed in! *Murder on the Orient Express*, *The Mousetrap*... even lots of modern ones, like -'

I'd heard enough. 'Don't be silly. We'll have our snow day today and everything will be back to normal tomorrow. We're not even snowed in yet, we'll be fine.'

We were in fact soon snowed in; deep snow surrounded our cliff hidden seaside village, and no one could get in or out. We weren't fine and everything wasn't back to normal tomorrow. There were two dead bodies that day and there was no one to investigate them in person but me: a mere school librarian, an amateur with an interest in murder mysteries.

I told you everyone always remembers a snow day.

2

'That Vicar and his cronies, they think they run this village!'

'Mum, come away from the window, stop staring at them.'

'Why not? You're staring out of the other window.'

It's true, I was. Mum had insisted I spend the morning of snow day in our family pub, The Chalk Inn, so she 'could make sure I was okay.' But my other offer was to go sledging down West Cliff path with my housemate Patrick. As I looked longingly through the glass at all of the people having fun down the cliff slope behind the pub, I wondered if I'd made the right decision.

'Just look at them, Edward. All that snow and they're still out there flogging their lukewarm mulled wine and their dodgy bratwursts. We'll never get any customers to come in and warm up in here while they're peddling their wares outside.'

Mum's view at the other side of the pub was of the village square, where the winter market was set up. The market was, as Mum so delicately put it, ran by our Vicar 'and his cronies.'

Chalk Gap Church was at the far side of the square to our pub, and has always been used by Reverend Flowers for various church events, including his very popular winter market from December through to mid-February. The village square is public and doesn't belong to the church land as such, but it had been so long linked to the church that no one ever objected to such use.

Well, almost no one objected. Mum googled legal ways of stopping him every time she got annoyed about it, which looked likely to be today. 'Why have they even opened this morning? We've got more than a foot of snow already. It'll serve them right if they all get stranded there.'

I didn't point out her flawed logic that the pub was also open in the snow, and that her objection was based on the market supposedly stealing customers.

'Who's out there?' I regretted asking this as soon as the words left my mouth. I didn't even need to know the answer. I knew which stalls were on the market; I walked through the village square at least once a week to visit my family. I also knew the market was depleted today, but had heard enough of Mum's rants about the Vicar's 'cronies' to take a wild guess who'd be keeping him company despite snowfall.

'Who do you think's out there? The usual lot – you know you only get a spot on that market if you're mates with the Reverend. Come and have a look.'

I sighed and saddled over to the window. I looked out to see about half a dozen of the twelve traditional wooden huts in the square open, an array of reds, greens and festive lights, despite Christmas having been and gone (they deliberately called it 'Winter Market' rather than specify Christmas, so they could extend it beyond December).

The snow across the square looked quite deep already, and there were no browsers in sight. Reverend Flowers and a group of women stood huddled next to the *Flowers' Flowers* hut, wrapped in hats, scarves and gloves, and nursing hot drinks in plastic cups. The Reverend himself was covering his bald head with a bright yellow beanie hat worn with a matching snood, both of which either belonged to his teenage son or he'd ill advisedly worn to try and look younger. A purple ski jacket and big blue snow boots completed his mismatching winter ensemble. Not that the circle around him seemed to mind. Even in this small huddle, you could see he was holding court with the group hanging on his every word.

'The vicar surrounded by all the women, there's a surprise!' Mum remarked over my shoulder. Allan Flowers certainly had a reputation for being very friendly with his female parishioners, and there'd been rumours round the village for years about his various supposed dalliances. His female volunteers even ran the church's market stall for him, selling homemade crafts and knick-knacks. None of them seemed to be around this morning but they often weren't when Frances was there.

'To be fair, Mum, one's his wife.' Frances Flowers was a grey, grubby, rat-like woman in her fifties, who in contrast to her husband was wearing dull, dark clothes which made her blend even further into the background. She ran *Flowers' Flowers* on the high street, and her business was always a centrepiece of the winter market.

'The rest aren't though, are they?' Mum retorted. 'And before you say, I know those two are a couple. Like that would stop the Reverend.'

'Those two' were Kimmy and Claire Atkinson, the owners of the village B&B and close friends of Allan and Frances Flowers. Kimmy was a large, jolly woman whose voice boomed out before her and who wore patterned knitted jumpers whatever the weather. Her wife, Claire, was smaller, quieter and more feminine, and always seemed the shrewder of the two; she was certainly the business mind of the pair. Their contribution to the market was a hut selling fresh cakes and pastries, which they baked in their B&B behind the square.

'And look at her, mutton dressed as lamb, as usual. When will she realise she can't compete with that young thing?'

'Her' was Gloria Hernandez, the most glamorous of the group in her leopard print matching hat and gloves and black velvet winter jacket. I was sure I'd be able to smell her perfume from where I stood if there wasn't a window between us. Gloria runs her own online sweet shop *Sweets For Your Sweet*, but each winter her .com business becomes a real, physical market stall for a couple of months.

Gloria is English but her surname belongs to her ex-husband Pedro, who was also a member of Reverend Flowers' social group until Pedro betrayed Gloria for 'that young thing' Cherry McDonald, who was half his age and a waitress in *Pedro's* restaurant. Sides were soon firmly picked and Pedro lost out. In more ways than one, as it was well known locally that his restaurant had been on the downturn in the last year: likely due to his adulterous reputation.

Pedro runs the imaginatively titled *Pedro's* and had been allowed to keep his hut at the winter market selling paella and mulled wine (although Mum told me it had seen hardly any business), but that was the only link he had now to his former friends. It didn't surprise me that he wasn't present this morning.

'And don't start me on that young chancer who's appeared at the market this year.' My eyes went over to where Mum was looking – the one oddity among the matching festive huts, a green van with the large red sign *Burger She Wrote* emblazoned on it. I had to give the stranger credit for the word play with the name; Noah had excitedly started planning all kinds of fast food related murder mysteries when he first saw it.

'They're not even real burgers, it's vegan only,' Mum added as I looked over at the hipster-looking man in his thirties sat in the burger van. His golden hair fell effortlessly out of his neat blue beanie hat, matching his beard. He seemed engrossed by his phone and was paying no attention to Flowers and his harem stood nearby.

'He's a good looking lad, I'll give him that much. Mind, I'm not the only one who thinks so.' Mum added. 'Someone needs to tell Reverend Flowers *that's* how you pull off one of them beanie hats. Probably not the only thing he's been pulling off, I'll bet.'

As Mum salivated over the potential gossip, it was then I noticed a sign on the burger van that I knew Mum shouldn't see. I had to get her out of the window.

'Anyway Mum, should we have a drink?' I offered as I tried to usher her away. But it was too late.

'Wait a minute, why the hell are they selling craft beer?' Oh dear. I knew my family and Reverend Flowers had always agreed they wouldn't sell any alcohol on the market, apart from mulled wine ('They're welcome to it – stupid novelty drink, I can't be bothered keeping it warmed up').

'I'm sure there's an explanation, Mum,' I said, attempting to keep her calm.

'Oh, I'm sure there is! Let's find out what it is, shall we? I'm going to see what Reverend Flowers has to say for himself.'

And with that, Mum flew out of the pub. God help the Reverend.

3

'Excuse me, Vicar! I want a word with you!' Mum barked from the pub doorway, as soon as we'd barely made it outside. Her voice carried through the cold air as I saw Kimmy nudge Claire with a knowing look, while Gloria shot Mum a glare as icy as the weather.

Reverend Flowers smiled at the women around him as he stepped forward from them, keeping his composure despite Mum's tone. 'Yes, Mrs Crisp, how may I be of help?'

'Don't you "Mrs Crisp" me. You 'may be of help' by explaining -'

'By explaining what exactly you've been doing with my girlfriend!'

That wasn't Mum's voice. The owner of the voice shot across the square in front of us, colliding with Flowers as he grabbed him by the neck, sending them both crashing to the floor. It was only once they were on the ground I realised it was Pedro Hernandez.

Everything from then seemed to happen in a blur. Someone screamed – I think Frances Flowers.

Someone shouted 'get off him, you idiot!' – probably Gloria Hernandez to her ex-husband. Someone cheered – almost definitely Mum. But what I was definitely sure of: several pair of eyes all on me, expecting me to do something.

I remember last year when a fight broke out in the school library between two boys. They were sixteen and both taller than me already, but I was the only adult in the room so I was expected to break it up. I had no idea what to do; I went into panic mode. Apparently, I shouted out 'someone stop them!' before a girl took me up on the offer and accidentally ended up being hit in the face. Her parents complained that I put her in danger.

There were no parents to complain this time, but I didn't want to endanger others again by not acting. I stepped forward as Pedro had Flowers by his ski jacket, repeatedly slamming him into the ground below him. I only realised afterwards that the thick snow underneath them would have cushioned the blow a little. At the time, I just knew I had to do something.

'Excuse me Pedro, can you get off him now please?'

'Oh, get out of the way, Edward,' I felt someone push me aside as I saw Mum dart forward and grab Pedro from behind. 'Alright you, that's enough!'

'I'm going to kill him!' Pedro moaned as he stumbled around with Mum clung to him like she was about to perform the Heimlich manoeuvre.

'No you're not, you moron, go home!' Gloria barked to her ex-husband as she stood blocking his path to the dazed Reverend Flowers, who Kimmy and Claire were helping to his feet. I noticed that Frances was stood rooted to the spot, her face frozen in terror.

'He's been sleeping with Cherry,' Pedro blurted out as he struggled under Mum's grasp.

'I have most certainly not,' Flowers managed as he attempted to brush snow off himself. The snow was still falling thick and fast and looked so peaceful around us, creating a bizarre atmosphere among the chaos.

'No one in their right mind would sleep with Cherry!' Gloria said as she moved forward to Pedro. 'Now get out of here before I call the police.'

'I'm not actually sure the police will be able to get through,' I said before I realised I'd spoken. The snow was falling rapidly and was predicted to get much worse later on that day; the road to our village off the main road would almost certainly be blocked soon, if not already.

'I'll deal with him myself then,' Gloria said menacingly, as she looked at her former husband straight in the eyes.

'Okay, okay, I'm going,' Pedro replied, as he shrugged Mum off him and brushed himself down.

But then we heard a blood-curdling scream from behind us. What now?

We all turned towards the church, where the noise came from, to see Jacob Flowers running in our direction. I noticed that the church path was the only place in view that had been cleared of snow.

'Leave my dad alone!' Jacob screamed as he hurtled towards us. Mum was on the ball straight away, moving towards Jacob to stop him, along with Kimmy who was the nearest side of Reverend Flowers to the church.

In contrast, Frances Flowers remained frozen to the spot, but with a bigger look of terror on her face. And Gloria simply stepped aside to clear the path to Pedro, evidently wanting him to get attacked. Jacob was a lanky, pale eighteen year old with greasy dyed black hair and a distinctly goth look. Despite his rage, he couldn't look menacing if he tried.

Almost to prove that point, as he reached the end of the church path and came on to the square, his feet went from under him. He moved through the air before landing in a heap on the thick snow below. 'For god's sake!' he cursed, picking up a ball of snow and throwing it in Pedro's direction.

'Do not use the Lord's name in vain!' Reverend Flowers said to his son, speaking for the first time since the incident started. He stood up straight and stepped forward, as if he'd visibly decided to take control of the situation. 'Let's put a stop to this little kerfuffle, shall we?'

He waited for everyone to stop still and look at him, commanding us like he did his congregation on Sundays. 'You,' he said first to Pedro. 'Get out of here, and don't come back. I'm sure you'll agree it's for the best if you don't continue on our market for the rest of winter.'

'Fine, whatever,' Pedro snapped back. 'But you haven't heard the last of this, *Reverend*. Oh, and Jacob? You're fired.' With one last look of disdain, he turned and started to wade his way though the deep snow.

'Yes, off you go!' shouted Gloria after him.

'Thank you, Gloria,' Flowers said firmly, in a way that told her that was enough. He turned to his teenage son, who was now back on his feet and looking particularly surly. 'Jacob, please help your mother look after the market for a while, so I can take these ladies in for a cup of tea, they've had quite the shock.'

Both Jacob and Frances nodded obediently, and moved back towards the festive huts. Why was Frances being made to stay outside and not be included in the 'ladies' who needed a cup of tea? The poor woman looked more shocked and upset than anyone.

But that seemed to barely matter to the Reverend, who had started to usher Gloria, Kimmy and Claire towards the church house. Glancing over his shoulder, he added, 'Linda and Edward, thank you for your help. We'll be fine from here.'

As they disappeared from view, the hipster guy from the *Burger She Wrote* van appeared, kicking snow out of his way to join us. I noticed his muscular arms under his thin cotton jumper; he would have been the ideal person to help with the Pedro incident.

'Is everything okay, guys? Can I help at all?'

'You could have about five minutes ago,' Mum snapped. 'Honestly, Edward, men are useless.'

I was just debating whether she expected an answer to that before she spoke to him again. 'Actually, you *can* help, if you want to make yourself useful. Stay here with young Jacob and keep an eye on the market, while I take Frances into the pub for a cup of tea.'

Frances looked at Mum in surprise, her face still pale and sorrowful. 'Me?'

'Yes, love. Why should you stay outside in the cold when you've had a nasty shock? Come on in, you can tell me all about it.'

Not taking no for an answer, Mum put her arm round Frances and started to lead her into the pub.

4

'So now, the Vicar is going to get murdered. I can't wait!'

If you haven't read my account of the real murder case Noah and I were involved in a few months ago, you may be a bit shocked by his comment. But otherwise, you know exactly what he's like and will know he doesn't mean it in a harmful way.

'I told you, Noah, we're not doing this again.' I was in my family's flat upstairs from the pub, making cups of tea for Mum and Frances. Of course, Mum could easily have made their drinks downstairs, but I knew she thought she'd be able to get more gossip out of the Vicar's wife if they had a few minutes alone.

'Obviously Pedro will be the number one suspect, but it will be more complex than that,' Noah continued happily. 'We'll have to start interviewing the suspects. Hopefully your Mum's made a good start with Mrs. Flowers.'

I sighed deeply as I gathered the drinks onto a tray and gave Noah some biscuits to carry. Bless him, I knew he couldn't help it, but we'd been here before. And although there was a reason his murderous predictions were correct last time, the thought of it happening again worried me.

'She's just making sure she's okay, I'm sure.' I knew that wasn't strictly true. Mum would be trying to find out every last piece of juicy gossip she could and Pedro's accusations were true or not. I was unsure what to expect as Noah and I carried the tea and biscuits into the pub.

'Forget the tea, boys, she's gone.'

It turned out that Frances stayed in the pub a matter of minutes, making an excuse to Mum and scarpering almost immediately.

'It's as if she's got something to hide,' Mum complained. 'She probably went straight home to question her husband. Mind you, I would. If I could prise him away from all those women around him.'

'Do you think the Vicar and Pedro's girlfriend are having an affair then?' Noah asked.

It was a good question. Claims like that don't normally come from nowhere, and as I've already mentioned, the Vicar's reputation goes before him. But I always thought that didn't go further than flirting with his female friends and parishioners to keep them on side.

Unfortunately, Mum answered first. 'Of course they were! There's no smoke without fire.'

To be fair, Cherry McDonald's reputation also goes before her. Half Pedro's age (in her early twenties), she started as a waitress at his restaurant while he was still married to Gloria, but the scandal of their affair ended the marriage in dramatic fashion.

I thought I better try and rescue the situation; Mum's speculation would only encourage Noah's murder theories. 'I've no idea, I doubt it. It was probably just a misunderstanding.'

I decided the best approach was to change the subject. 'Anyway, look at this snow. It's the biggest snow fall I've ever known us to have.'

That wasn't just an idle change of subject. The snow was falling thicker and faster with no end in sight; at this rate, the village would be cut off from the main road soon.

'Then there'll be no one to investigate the murder but us!' he said, clapping his hands together and sounding delighted. 'I bet the body is buried deep in the snow already.'

Again, I rushed to answer him before Mum could. 'What body? You just said you thought it was the Vicar. I only left him fifteen minutes ago, and he was in a group of people. Now I don't want to hear any more about anyone being murdered.'

'Okay, I'm sorry.' He stopped and looked down at the floor, leaving me feeling guilty. But he wasn't finished. 'Just one more thing though, and

I'm sorry, it is kind of to do with someone being murdered.'

I rolled my eyes. 'Go on.'

'It's more of a question really. I know I said it would be the Vicar who might get murdered, but has anyone seen Cherry McDonald this morning?'

5

Noah spent the next couple of hours looking at Cherry's social media profiles to look for any evidence that she'd been online – she hadn't, which fuelled his speculation that she was the murder victim (not that anyone else believed there *would* be a murder victim at that point). Mum, meanwhile, speculated that Cherry had instead ran off somehow with all of Pedro's money, firmly casting her in the 'young gold-digger' archetype.

But their guessing and gossip was soon forgotten, as the rest of the morning brought the biggest snowstorm our little village had ever seen. Generally, East Sussex gets much less snow than back in the North West where my family's from; in the twenty or so years we've lived down here, I can remember maybe half a dozen proper snowfalls. In contrast, every winter I recalled in Wigan when I was a child seemed like a magical parade of sledging, snowball fights and building snowmen – frozen toes and ice cold ears, then warming up in front of the fireplace afterwards.

This seemed to be something Mum was trying to recreate at the moment, as she made Dad put more coal on the fire in the pub while she encouraged everyone to gather round it.

'Come on everyone, come and get warm!' she shouted across the pub. 'Nothing like a proper fire to warm you up. Alfie and Dylan will have that fresh soup ready soon too. Don't worry, we'll sort you out here at the Chalk!'

Mum had managed to make the pub an impromptu community centre following the snowstorm, jumping on the idea before Reverend Flowers had the chance to offer up the church hall.

'Someone needs to do it and it might as well be us,' she'd said as soon as she realised how much the village would be disrupted. 'I'm sure the Vicar has his own problems to deal with anyway.'

Nobody had seen Reverend or Frances Flowers over the last couple of hours, even though the Flowers' harem of Gloria, Kimmy and Claire were amongst the helpers in the pub. The Chalk was a hive of activity, acting as a base for the volunteers who were shovelling snow, attempting to clear doorways, phoning vulnerable members of the community to check on them, and unsuccessfully trying to dig a route through to the rest of the village.

The scenes were unlike anything I'd ever known in my lifetime. Chalk Gap village was buried under mountains of snow, which was still falling relentlessly. I'd heard several comments –

mostly from Dad – that it was close to three feet deep, which if true would make it the worst UK snowfall since the infamous winter of 2010-11, ten years ago, when chaos reigned across the country. Bizarrely, Chalk Gap was barely affected by that, with the worst conditions passing our village by.

But not this time. Everything and everyone had been brought to a halt, with no discernible path from one part of the village to another. Our village centre at the foot of the cliffs, consisting of the southern end of the high street, village square and beach, was therefore cut off from the rest of Chalk Gap – with many people unable to wade through the snow to get home.

Then there were those who had come to help before the worst of the snow, or those who had deliberately stuck around to do what they could.

'You can't beat the community spirit in Chalk Gap,' Dad always says. Dad, of course, had used it as an excuse to get his pub disco set going, with the soundtrack of *Frozen* currently blasting through the pub, although most people ignored it as they went back and forth or sat keeping warm.

Further to Dad's comment, the community was fairly well represented. As well as Gloria from the sweet shop and Kimmy and Claire from the B&B, there was Annabelle King who ran the convenience store, the couple who had just taken over the café, and a guy who I recognised as the young police officer who guarded the staff room after Miss Finch was murdered. Even though we didn't have village police (we were far too small for that in these cost-cutting times), I remembered my colleague telling me at the time that he lived in the village.

Several of my colleagues from school were also present. My best friend and housemate Patrick Herrera, our new Science teacher Becky Lau, our caretaker Carol Fletcher and the school P.A. Dylan Spence, also now my brother Alfie's boyfriend; the two were currently in the pub kitchen preparing the soup Mum had mentioned. Technically, Alfie took over as pub landlord when my parents took early retirement from it, but at times like this you'd be surprised to discover that.

Meanwhile, Kat Parker, our Head Teacher and my close friend, seemed to have taken charge of the volunteers and was busy giving out tasks to them. I thought this may have caused a clash with Mum, until I realised that Mum was more bothered about the hosting part than the actual helping.

Kat had given us all various tasks in small groups, so Noah, Patrick, Jacob Flowers and I were now clearing the snow behind the pub at the foot of the cliff path, which Mum was pleased about; it apparently meant the sledgers would be more likely to come into the pub if they had a clear path.

The two teenagers were a few feet ahead of us: Jacob silent and sullen, with Noah jabbering away happily.

'All this snow is just so exciting, isn't it? I'll lend you my copy of *The Sittaford Mystery* if you like – everyone is snowed in but a murder takes place.' He looked around, taking in the winter wonderland surrounding us. 'It's just so atmospheric, the perfect setting for a murder!'

'It's alright,' Jacob muttered in reply, looking like he wanted to commit a murder of his own. Since Noah moved into the pub with Mum and Dad, I knew he'd been attempting to befriend Jacob. The vicar's son was a good year or so older than Noah, and having cast himself as an angst ridden goth, was quite a different character. And I'd never seen them interact with each other at school. But I could tell they shared being on the social outskirts of their age group, so maybe a friendship would develop after all.

'So you don't think she moved out because of me then?'

My own best friend, Patrick, was preoccupied while we shovelled snow. If you read my last account detailing Miss Finch's murder, you'll know that Kat and Patrick used to be in a relationship together, but settled instead on being friends and housemates (along with me). Since Kat's promotion to Head Teacher, she decided her house sharing days were over and has just bought a nice little cottage in the village. It seemed quite natural to do it and their relationship was so far in the past that I'd not even linked it to that. But Patrick had.

'I've told you a million times, of course not!' I stopped to get my breath. I was a lot shorter and a lot less stronger than Patrick, and the exertion of shovelling while wading through snow up to my knees was difficult.

'You don't think it's because of me and Becky then?' Patrick and Becky Lau had happened quite quickly. Becky had started working at school in September, and they were dating by October half term. It could have been potentially awkward for all concerned with Kat being their boss, but I wasn't sure Becky even knew about Kat and Patrick's past. To me, they're just my two best friends.

'Patrick, she's a school Head Teacher now. It makes sense she'd want her own place, she can afford it.' Knowing how independent Kat is, it was a surprise she'd stayed living with us as long as she had.

'I know that, buddy,' he replied as he dug through the snow in front of us. 'I just hope she's okay, that's all.' He looked like he was about to say something else, but instead he just focused on his task of shovelling. We went on in silence for a little while until it was broken suddenly.

'I swear to God, you better take that back right now!'

Jacob. His father wasn't around this time to tell him off for blaspheming. Patrick and I were going to have to deal with his current outburst, which at the moment involved threatening Noah with a shovel.

'What's going on?' Patrick asked immediately, quicker to react than I was. I was busy taking in the scene. Noah didn't seem overly scared that an angry young man was waving a shovel at him.

'He was saying things about Cherry, and my dad,' Jacob snarled in reply.

'Oh, is that what's upset you?' Noah said cheerfully. 'I'm sorry, I didn't mean anything by it. I only said that when there's a murder in a love triangle, it's interesting that the murder victim has usually done something wrong. Like how Linnet Ridgeway in *Death on the Nile* steals her best friend's fiancé before she gets murdered.'

I rolled my eyes. Noah's fascination with murder mysteries had got him in trouble yet again. 'Noah, now's not the time for that.'

'Oh no, it's fine,' he continued. 'I'm not saying Jacob's Dad has done anything wrong sleeping with the waitress, but when one of them gets murdered some people might think they deserve it.'

'That's it!' Jacob roared as he darted towards

Noah.

'JACOB!' I recognised the Vicar's voice before I saw him trying to wade through the snow, looking very much alive. I thought he'd simply come to prevent his son's second attack of the day, until I noticed the terrified look on his face.

'Gentlemen, I need your help. Something's happened at the vicarage.'

Noah, Patrick and I stopped and looked at Reverend Flowers. Jacob seemed unsure, looking uncertainly between his father and Noah, still holding the shovel in the air.

'What is it?' I asked.

'I'm afraid we need to ring for the police. It's my wife. She's dead.'

Jacob dropped the shovel into the snow and stared at his father. 'Dad, what did you say?'

Flowers looked at his son slowly, as if only just remembering he was with us. 'Oh, Jacob. Your mother. She's dead. I think she's been murdered.'

'I knew it! I knew there'd be a murder!' Noah clapped his gloved hands together. Luckily for him, Jacob Flowers was too much in shock or there might have been a second one.

6

Poor Frances Flowers seemed to have met her end in the back garden of the vicarage, which is situated behind the church away from the main square. She lay on her back just outside their kitchen doorway, her eyes closed, looking peaceful. She wore a dowdy knitted brown jumper but the outdoor jacket she wore earlier had gone. There was a patch of red in the snow under her head. I then noticed the snow all over her body and face; I guessed that her husband found her facing down and had since turned her over.

'I... I had to check on her you understand,' Reverend Flowers stammered, as if reading my mind.

'You should never move a dead body, it could affect the investigation,' Noah interjected.

We'd rang 999 and were waiting for the emergency services to figure out a way to get here. Patrick had taken Jacob inside the pub, while the Reverend showed me and Noah where he'd found his wife. I'd suggested us all waiting together at the pub, but Flowers insisted on taking us there. He probably needed someone else to see it, to feel it was real. Although bringing Noah along didn't seem like the best decision in hindsight, it was a better alternative to leaving him to upset Jacob further.

'I didn't even think of that, I just saw her lying there and I had to check she was okay.'

'But she wasn't,' Noah said, unnecessarily. Then he added, 'I'm really sorry for your loss, Vicar. Mrs. Flowers seemed like a nice lady.'

'She was, she was the best,' Flowers replied, while shivering. He looked at me and I could see the utter dismay on his face. 'Edward, who would do such a thing?'

'To answer that, we need to look at the crime scene,' Noah answered for me. 'Don't worry, we're good at that!'

'We'll leave that for the police, Noah,' I said quickly, feeling a strong sense of déjà vu. Yet there were several visual clues that left little doubt to even the most casual eye as to what happened.

A shovel lay in the snow just a couple of feet from Frances' body, the unforgiving steel edge a mix of ominous red and white. The snow in the vicarage garden was very deep, so that the footprints leading away from the body across the garden were easy to see, although I noticed the falling snow was already starting to cover them. They stopped at the six foot fence at the end of the property, which I imagined their owner had climbed to jump their way out of the vicarage grounds.

I had something to double check. 'The fence backs straight on to the bottom of the cliff, doesn't it?' I imagined it did; the pub backed on to the West Cliff and the vicarage was in roughly the same position in front of the East Cliff. The difference was the cliffs were in plain view from the pub, while the vicarage had a high fence in between.

'Yes, that's right,' Flowers confirmed.

'So the person escaping would be in full view of the people sledging down the cliff slope!' Noah said.

That's exactly what I was thinking too, hence the question, but I wasn't going to verbalise that thought at this point. Noah may have gone into detective mode, but a man had just lost his wife, and his son needed him.

'Thank you for showing us where you found her, Vicar. Let's get back to the pub and see Jacob. The police will know what to do next.'

I remember the next thing that happened being right on cue as I spoke those words, but in reality it might not have been that exact moment. My phone vibrated and I saw a name I hadn't seen for a few months: DI Jamie Appleby. My former school bully turned CID Detective Inspector led the last murder investigation in Chalk Gap, so it made sense that he would be involved in this one. What didn't make sense was why he was phoning me.

'Edward, mate! Good to speak to you,' he boomed down the phone as soon as I answered. 'Though I wish it was in better circumstances.'

'You mean the murder.'

I didn't know how much Appleby knew at this stage, but I felt immediate guilt at being caught at a murder scene once again. I braced myself for the telling off to the amateur interfering in police business. But the telling off didn't come.

'The thing is, mate, we're having a bit of trouble getting into the village. There's no getting through from the main road at the minute, not even on foot, let alone in a vehicle. We've got all the man power we have working on it, but it won't be easy.' I could see the problem. The village centre was almost a mile and a half from the A259 main road, down a relatively narrow country road which would be buried deep in snow.

I realised how I could help. 'You want me to get a group to start digging through at this end, is that it?' I knew that this was on Kat's task list, and several people were already assigned to this job. 'There's a few people already trying.'

'Thanks mate, I'm already on that but I don't think it will do much good. The snow's just too deep, the stretch is too long and the snow's falling faster than we can move it.'

'What are you going to do then?' I asked.

'We're working with the coastguard to see if we can access the village via boat or helicopter. But at the minute the sea is just too rough, and I don't think we'll be able to land the helicopter any-where in all this snow.' He paused. 'So I've had to come up with another plan.'

'Of course, what is it? I'll help whatever way I can, and I'm sure I can get lots of other people as well.'

'Well, you see mate, it's your help specifically I need. How do you fancy investigating another murder for me?'

7

'How can I be the one doing that?' I was careful not to say *investigating the murder* in front of Noah; his over-excited reaction wouldn't have been appropriate in front of Reverend Flowers. 'You've said it before – I'm a civilian, I'm not the police.'

I thought back to Miss Finch's murder. Yes, I'd been the one who'd eventually solved it, but my work consisted of me talking to my colleagues and friends on the side, mostly behind Appleby's back, while the official investigation was underway.

'You won't be the one doing it. At least not officially. We've got a uniformed constable who lives in the village. It's not ideal but he's going to be my proxy, with me leading the investigation virtually until we can get through.'

'You don't need me then, do you?' I ventured. As I spoke the words, I thought of the young officer amongst the volunteers earlier in the pub. That must have been who Appleby meant.

'Mate, PC Wood has been a cop for less than a couple of years. He's still wet behind the ears, he can't do it by himself.'

'It's a couple of years more experience than me,' I replied. I thought back to the day of Miss Finch's murder, with PC Wood (I didn't remember his name until now) guarding the staffroom door, bored and uninterested, playing with his phone most of the time. And how easily one of my colleagues had manipulated him into letting us leave.

'Honestly Edward, he's useless. I'd rather not use him, but the DCI's over-ruled me. Says if we've got an officer in the village that's the only option until we get through. He's only okayed it 'cos he thinks it won't be too long. But PC Wood is a beat cop, he can't investigate a murder. I'm just gonna have him do all the practical stuff – preserving the scene and so on. You'll be doing the real work.'

I looked at the scene in front of me while I was on the phone. Noah had moved closer to me, quite blatantly trying to listen to the call. Reverend Flowers had knelt down by his wife in silence, his head bowed. He seemed to be praying.

There was something about the way the Vicar was bowed in prayer that moved me. He deserved to know what had happened to his wife, and it surely wouldn't be long until the police found their way through the village by land, sea or air.

'Okay, I'll do it.'

'Good man, I knew you would,' Appleby said heartedly. I could imagine him shaking my hand firmly or even slapping my back if he was here in person. 'I'll brief Wood – like I said, he'll do all the official stuff, you just do your usual thing – talking to the right people, asking the right questions, general poking your nose in.'

I should have known he couldn't resist a dig, even when asking for my help. Appleby always saw himself as the alpha, and I was surprised he was relinquishing control, to me of all people, as much as he was. But I supposed he didn't have much choice.

I still had a million questions about this strange situation. 'Does your DCI know I'm involved, surely not? Won't PC Wood just report back straight away?'

Appleby scoffed at this. 'Not if I tell him not to, he won't. Mate, I'm the DI, he'll do whatever I say. I'm still the SIO on the case, just remotely for now, that's all. And obviously, your part is completely unofficial, yeah. As far as this investigation goes, you don't exist.'

I sniffed at Appleby's cocky, straight to the point manner. I probably imagined that he enjoyed those last three words a little too much. I felt them and it did hurt me a little. I wouldn't call us friends as such these days, but he obviously trusted me to involve me like this yet his ego was still very much there.

'Okay then, what do you need me to do?' The

Vicar had stood up again and was looking over at me; I was eager to get back to him before Noah started up another conversation.

'Wood's Sergeant is briefing him as we speak. He's going to come and secure the crime scene, then we're going to need two trustworthy volunteers to guard it. I want you to do that for me please – send them to Wood at the scene once I give you the nod. I suggest the Spanish guy, your mate Patrick, as one. And I thought he could have that Noah kid with him.'

'Noah?' I exclaimed from my end of the conversation. Noah himself jumped to life, looking expectant and excited. I lowered my voice and trudged a few steps through the snow. 'You want Noah guarding a crime scene?' I whispered.

'Think about it, mate. Think what he was like last time. He'll be following you round, trying to investigate everyone himself. This way he's in one place, got one of his teachers with him, and thinks he's got a really important job so he'll dedicate himself to it.'

I'd previously had issues with Appleby's thoughts on Noah, but I had to admit, this was quite a clever plan. But then I thought about everything Noah went through in the Miss Finch investigation, and his stunning bravery. Despite his unusual approach (acting as if we're all murder mystery characters), he was actually an asset. I wanted him more involved; I wanted him helping me.

'It's okay, Appleby, he'll get bored too easily doing that, I'll find a use for him that still keeps him out of trouble. And Patrick will be busy helping Kat co-ordinate the snowstorm volunteers.' I thought of the best pair I knew to guard the scene. 'I could get Alfie and Dylan to do it?'

'Your brother and his fella, the school P.A. guy? Perfect, they're reliable.'

'Great, I'll ask them both,' I confirmed. 'Then what?'

'One of my team is on to your local GP, Doctor Albright, isn't it? We're hoping she can get through from the high street to work with our Pathologist to confirm the death and hopefully the time. Then once that's done and the crime scene is secure, I want PC Wood to set up a temporary incident room near the scene. Somewhere private I can brief you both when I need to.'

I thought. The pub was already in use as the impromptu snowstorm hub, and would be likely to have Mum over my shoulder at every turn. But that left the church hall free – a suggestion Appleby was happy with.

'Perfect, mate. Really close to the crime scene, and if me and Wood end up having to formally question any of them, we can have them there and I'll do it remotely from here. They'll all feel comfortable enough in the church hall to let their guard down.'

I felt my heartbeat quicken at the mention of *they'll all*. I realised that once again the villagers of Chalk Gap would be under the investigation spotlight: my friends and neighbours as murder suspects. I couldn't believe this was happening again.

'Okay, so I'll give you half an hour or so,' Appleby confirmed. 'Then we'll do a video call briefing – me, you and Wood. You can tell me what you know and we'll get a plan of action going. Hopefully it won't be too long after that we'll be able to get through to the village somehow.'

I'm sure he wasn't as hopeful they'd get through soon as I was. Even with a successfully solved murder under my belt, I'd never felt more out of depth in my life.

8

As I led Reverend Flowers into the Chalk Inn, I was conscious that everything felt different to an hour ago. Do you ever get the sensation that you don't quite feel like you're in reality, like everything around you is being performed by actors in a play? Maybe it's the way my brain works. Especially after it's had a shock, which seems to be happening more frequently lately.

'Oh, Vicar!' Mum shrieked across the pub as she ran towards us and threw her arms around him. 'I'm so, so sorry.' If everyone around me *were* actually actors in a movie, Mum definitely considered herself the leading lady.

'I, erm, I... don't know what to say,' Flowers stammered as Gloria, Kimmy and Claire made their way over and embraced him.

'Where is my son?' He asked as he separated himself from the group hug. Kimmy gestured over to the fireplace, where Jacob sat staring at the dancing flames. Patrick was sat with him but he was in a world of his own.

'Don't you worry, Vicar,' Mum called out as he

headed over to Jacob. 'My Edward will find out who did this! He's working with the police.'

I felt several eyes in the room on me. How did Mum even know this yet? I realised exactly how when I noticed the one pair of eyes looking away sheepishly, belonging to Noah. This was a rare moment of self-awareness for him, but he did have a strong sense of right and wrong. He probably felt guilty for listening in to my call then repeating it.

'Let's get a table, buddy,' Patrick called to me, as he left Jacob's table to give him and his father some privacy.

Although Mum didn't give them the same courtesy, suddenly needing to stoke the fire right next to them. 'I'll keep my eye on him for you, Edward, don't worry,' she whispered to me as she went. 'I've seen enough true crime documentaries to know what's going on here. It's always the husband.'

Kat, who had just finished sending the next group out with shovels, glanced over at us.

'You need a break, Kat, come sit down!' Patrick shouted to her before she could busy herself with something else. 'Alfie and Dylan are over there, let's join them.'

Kat sighed before nodding to her head and moving towards Alfie and Dylan, while we did the same. I was aware of Noah looking over at us, as if waiting for something.

'Come on then, Noah, come and join us,' I said as I grinned at him. I couldn't let him miss out if I was updating everyone on Appleby's request. Even though he'd clearly already heard my end of the conversation.

'Oh thank you, I didn't want to intrude without being asked!' He said as he bounded over to the group. It didn't usually stop him, but he must have still felt guilty for blabbing to Mum.

As he sat down, I could feel someone else watching. As I looked across the bar, Becky Lau, who appeared to be washing cups (God knows how Mum roped her into that one), quickly looked down. She clearly did know about Kat and Patrick's past; she must have been wondering why Patrick had asked his ex-girlfriend to come and sit with us, but not her. It was a good question.

It was that same ex-girlfriend who saved his bacon as he remained oblivious to the situation. 'Becky, over here!' Kat beckoned across the room. 'You've worked your socks off all morning, come and have a break with us.' Becky looked pleased and I was glad there was no friction between the two women. Of course, Kat was Becky's boss too, but I was happy there was no girlfriend /ex-girlfriend stand-off between them.

In addition to Becky, I remember thinking I was surrounded by my closest confidantes, my support network: my two long-term best friends, my brother, and his partner – also our colleague and Kat's P.A. – who was becoming a good friend of mine in his own right.

The five of us had become a quite close group since the Miss Finch case; Alfie and Dylan having separate connections to the group made them a perfect fit to socialise with us, and it seemed to work well for everyone.

Alfie wasn't quite as much as a workaholic and was stepping back a bit from the pub, letting Mum and Dad take the reins again a bit more (which they both clearly loved); Dylan had a group of friends in the village after moving here; Patrick and Kat seemed much more comfortable hanging out together as part of a larger group; and we still got to see Kat since she moved out of our house. As for me, my social life was developing beyond once a week Friday night outings to karaoke. And I quite liked it.

And of course, I mustn't forget Noah in this. As a 17 year old and a post-16 student at our school, he wasn't part of our social group as such – Kat and Patrick (as his Head Teacher and English teacher respectively) in particular had to keep an element of professional distance from him. But he was a part of mine and Alfie's family now, and more than ever he was one of my absolute favourite people. So no one ever minded if he came to join us with a lemonade when we were all in the pub together.

But he still hadn't quite grasped all of the social norms of mixing in a group. 'Edward, would you like me to take the minutes of our meeting?' he asked as he produced his phone and went into the notes app.

It had taken me weeks after Noah moved in with Mum and Dad to stop calling me 'Sir,' as he was expected to in school. But I still hadn't managed to stop him from minuting our conversations in his phone, in case they were useful in an 'investigation.'

'It's okay, Noah, I think we can all just listen to Edward's story for now,' Kat said gently but authoritatively. Everyone listened while I quietly told them exactly what Appleby said and what he wanted me to do, including our idea for Alfie and Dylan to guard the scene, which they agreed to.

'I'm so glad we're investigating another murder!' Noah exclaimed as he waved his arms in delight.

'Ssshh!' I spat out in a panic, as I glanced across the pub to where the Flowers men were sat consoling each other. They were a few tables away and luckily they didn't seem to hear. Even luckier, neither did Mum, who was now 'cleaning' the mantle-piece over the fireplace right next to them.

'Oh yes, sorry!' Noah said a fraction quieter than the first time, as he reached for his beloved phone. 'Can I make some notes now?'

'Not yet, buddy,' Patrick said this time. 'We're not going to talk about it in that much detail yet.' He was right. It didn't seem fair to talk about the ins and outs of the murder with the victim's husband and son sat in the same room as us.

'Of course, we won't know the details until Doctor Albright confirms the death!' Noah still seemed to misunderstand exactly why we couldn't talk in depth yet, seeming to think it was due to a lack of medical detail.

'Bev sent me a message, she'll be at the scene by now,' Kat replied. Doctor Beverley Albright was Kat's cousin, which always made me slightly self-conscious when discussing my mental health with my GP. 'She'll do what she can, but it won't be the same as having the Pathologist there.'

'I can't believe they still can't get through,' Dylan said. 'Still, it's a pleasant surprise, Appleby asking you to look into it.'

A surprise? Yes. Pleasant? I wasn't sure. Another round of interrogating and suspecting people I know, with the expectation I'm going to be able to solve it, just because I'm a murder mystery enthusiast. I was worried I'd be put off reading them altogether at this rate.

'Do you think you can trust him?' Patrick asked as he played with the beermat in front of him. 'You two sure have a complex history.'

We did. My old school bully was very wary of me in the Miss Finch case, not wanting me to pry too much, though he seemed grateful when I managed to identify the murderer. I wondered how much his colleagues and superiors knew about my involvement then, and noted that my support this time was being kept under wraps.

'To be fair, I've been dealing with him on the phone just now, he was really nice,' Kat piped up.

'What do you mean, you've been dealing with him?' Patrick asked, throwing the beermat down and earning himself an odd glance from Becky next to him.

'Yeah, we've been liaising about the snowstorm problem,' she replied cheerfully. 'Obviously I'm co-ordinating volunteers at this end, and he's got police and various others at that end trying to get through, so we're hoping we might meet in the middle.'

'I think it will be hours until they get through, if today at all. It's not going anywhere and it's still falling.' I glanced through the window at the depths of snow surrounding us. The formerly beautiful winter wonderland now held an eerie, sinister feel to it, as if it was a co-conspirator harbouring a murderer. I kept picturing the sharp white snow with Frances Flowers' dark red blood in it.

As I thought about this, Reverend Flowers and Jacob stood up from their table and we all pretended not to watch (some of us better than others) as the Vicar gently led his son out of the pub. A few seconds of respectful silence followed, before it was broken – I don't think I need to tell you by who.

'Can we talk about the murder properly now, please?'

I sighed at Noah's request, but noticed the expectant expressions on every face at the table. Our Vicar's wife being murdered in the snow was huge, shocking news; it was natural for everyone to want to discuss the details and make sense of it. And I was about to become involved, like it or not, so the input of my friends would be welcomed.

'Okay then. I don't even know where to start from.'

'How about what happened in the square this morning?' Dylan ventured. 'I only know half of the story but I'm sure that's important.'

He was right; I'd been thinking along these lines myself. Thinking logically, it couldn't be a coincidence that the Vicar was involved in a public confrontation before he found his wife dead a couple of hours later. Those two events must have been connected somehow.

'Yes, that's a good idea,' I agreed. 'So, Mum and I went out to the square -'

'Wait! *Now* can I take notes?'

Everyone looked at Noah and I laughed, nodding my head. His enthusiasm might seem inappropriate at times but his way of looking at things could be helpful, and I knew what he'd write would be thorough. I agreed and went on to tell the story of Pedro attacking Reverend Flowers.

I finished the story and was surprised to see Becky, the newcomer to our grouping, be the first one to speak. 'So, you basically need to know whether Pedro's accusation of the Reverend sleeping with Cherry is true. If so, your killer is probably Reverend Flowers or Pedro.'

'Yes, but I'd go back a step before that first, and think about who was there on the scene and what their involvement was.' Kat's contribution earned her a look from Becky, who then smiled quickly to cover it.

'I agree with both those things!' Noah called out as he typed away quickly in his phone. Both points did make sense. Of course, if the Vicar *was* having an affair it would likely link directly to his wife's death; it could have been in a marital argument, or Pedro could have gone to confront Reverend Flowers again in an angry rage. So, of course they were prime suspects.

Although Kat was right. The two separate occurrences of the fight and the murder seemed connected, like a cause and effect. One happened because of the other. But not necessarily involving the two main parties in the fight; the incident in the square happened with a number of witnesses and people present, and something or someone there likely led to Frances' death.

'Me too, Noah, but Kat has a point; let's note everyone who was present this morning.' Becky looked crestfallen at my comment, which made me nervous for a second. I tried to compose myself by focusing on Noah. 'Will you note these names down for me?'

He clapped his hands in triumph before starting typing away. 'So obviously we have Reverend Flowers and Pedro. And I'd probably say Jacob too.'

'A teenage boy killing his mum, that's a bit dark, isn't it?' Becky commented.

Noah considered her carefully and then smiled.

'What you need to know about murder mysteries is suspect everyone; don't leave anybody out. It could be the person you least expect. Agatha Christie had a little girl killer once.'

Referencing his classic mystery tropes was something I knew no one would mind him doing; the outcome of Miss Finch's murder had shocked all of us. Expressing this through his knowledge of murder mysteries came naturally for Noah, and it didn't surprise me to see him including his friend Jacob on the list.

'Okay, so who else do we have?' Kat said, moving the conversation along.

'Everyone else there is in the Flowers' friendship group, really,' I clarified as I fidgeted with my hands. 'Claire and Kimmy Atkinson, and Gloria Hernandez.'

'Were any of *them* having an affair with the Vicar?' Becky asked. She seemed keen to be involved in the conversation.

'Obviously not Claire and Kimmy,' Noah replied quickly and loudly. 'They're lesbians!'

Alfie and Dylan both looked at each other and burst out laughing. 'Yeah, it reduces their odds a little,' Dylan said through chuckles.

'And we're friends with them,' Alfie added. 'They're alright.'

'Well, I didn't know,' Becky snapped.

'Of course you didn't, baby.' Patrick put his arm round her to comfort her.

It's a really good point, though,' Kat said. 'Just because Pedro accused the Vicar and Cherry, doesn't mean they were the ones having the affair. That's what I meant about thinking of everyone.'

'Yes, exactly, thank you Kat,' Becky replied through a smile. I couldn't quite work out was going on with these two women, but it now seemed that Kat was aware of Becky being the outsider and was trying to include her.

'So Gloria could be having an affair with Reverend Flowers!' Noah announced loudly. I looked around in panic to check if Gloria was in hearing distance, but she was no longer in the pub.

Gloria Hernandez was definitely someone worth talking to regardless. As well as being the Flowers' best friend, she was Pedro's very bitter ex-wife and had been the most vocal against him during the incident. She was bound to have insight, however biased, as to what had been happening.

'That's the sweet hut lady, isn't it?' Dylan said. 'I love her strawberry bon-bons.'

'Who else? Kat asked, again getting the conversation back on track. 'Are we missing anyone?'

'Mum's always gossiping about the Vicar and his lady parishioners,' Alfie said. 'Any chance one of them got jealous and did in their love rival?'

It was far-fetched, but any explanation of who killed the meek wife of the Vicar seemed far-fetched. So it was possible.

Kat answered before I got a chance to. 'Maybe, but I meant sticking with the people at the scene this morning. Was there anyone else there, Ed?'

'Well, me and Mum were, obviously,'

'That's it, I knew it!' Alfie said dramatically. 'Obviously Mum saw her opportunity to strike revenge on the Flowers for daring to sell craft beer out there.'

'Don't even joke about that,' I said as I sighed warily, before realising something. 'That's it, the craft beer! I almost forgot – the *Burger She Wrote* guy. He was there too, but he only came over at the end. I didn't think much at the time, but I suppose it was strange he didn't come and help stop Pedro.'

'You think he could be something to do with it, buddy?' Patrick asked me.

'I don't know, but he's definitely worth speaking to. Mum always says how the winter market is so close knit, I wonder how he even got a spot there. Maybe he knows Reverend Flowers.'

'The mysterious stranger!' Noah said. 'They're

always a good suspect.'

'Yes,' I agreed. 'I'll just need to find out a bit about who he is.'

'His name is Everest Brown, he's 37, he's from London, but he's staying in Kimmy and Claire's B&B while he's here.'

I looked back at Noah in amazement. 'How do you know all that?'

'Oh, I asked him. He was very a nice man actually. But that doesn't fool me, he could still be the killer. Remember Hercule Poirot said "every murderer is someone's old friend."'

I caught myself laughing out loud, while everyone else on the table smiled politely. Despite the seriousness of the situation, it felt strangely good to be doing this with Noah again, and his unique interpretations always made me smile. 'That's fantastic, Noah, thank you.'

He beamed back at me before replying. 'So we're kind of looking at a closed circle mystery, but it's a bigger circle this time.'

Everyone at the table looked perplexed. 'How's that, Noah?' my brother was the one to ask.

Noah sat up proudly, his shoulders back and his head up. He was loving this. 'Our core group of suspects are the people who were present in the square this morning: Reverend Flowers,

Jacob Flowers, Pedro Hernandez, Gloria Hernandez, Kimmy Atkinson, Claire Atkinson, Everest Brown.'

'So you have seven suspects?' Becky asked.

'Yes, and no,' he replied. 'They are seven *possible* suspects. But like we said, it could easily be a jealous parishioner, or someone we don't know about, or even Cherry McDonald.'

He was right. 'Yes, Noah. She wasn't there in the square, but she was the subject of the argument. She easily could have gone to the Vicarage and got into a row with Frances.'

'Exactly,' he continued. 'So it isn't a closed circle mystery in that sense, as it could be someone other than those people. But it is a closed circle mystery. Like I said, just a much bigger circle.'

I knew all about closed circle mysteries, but even I was getting confused now. 'What do you mean, Noah?'

I saw him take a breath as he paused dramatically. He was loving this. 'When Frances Flowers left the pub earlier, very much alive, the snow was already getting too thick to get out of the village. And now, no one can get in, but no one can get out either. Chalk Gap *is* the closed circle. Even if it isn't one of those seven, the murderer is definitely someone still in the village.'

9

'Hi, I'm Dean Wood, PC Wood. Nice to meet you and pleased to be working with you.'

I don't think I've ever had my hand shook as enthusiastically as I did in that moment. I'd just arrived at the makeshift incident room in the church hall, and the young constable had come bounding over, looked me straight in the eye and beamed at me, while clasping my hand and shaking it rigorously. The whole routine was as if it had been practised to perfection.

'Nice to see you again,' I replied as he looked confused in return. 'We have met before. You were guarding the school staffroom in the Miss Finch case. And I was there when you made the arrest.'

'Oh yes, mate, yes. I remember you now.' He had no poker face, and it was clear from his expression he didn't know who I was. 'Nasty business that, wasn't it, mate?'

'Yes, it was,' I agreed, before realising another way he might know me: how most people in the village know me. 'By the way, my family run the Chalk Inn, the village pub. You might know me from there.'

'Ah, I don't go in there. Too old a crowd for me – no offence, mate, of course. I prefer going to the clubs in Eastbourne or Brighton. You know how it is, mate.'

I resisted rolling my eyes. Another officer like Appleby, who thinks they're everyone's 'mate.' Is that part of their training or what? As I took him in though, my first impression was he didn't have the sharpness of Appleby. He certainly seemed keen, but this excitable puppy of a man looked naïve and, well, *young*. I noted earlier that I felt out of my depth, but if I was in the shallow end of the pool with my armbands, PC Wood was in the kiddies' pool in a rubber ring.

I gestured to Alfie and Dylan who were behind me. 'These are the two volunteers who DI Appleby has asked to guard the crime scene.'

He looked at them as if he'd only just noticed that I had two other people with me. 'Hello, fellas.'

'PC Wood, this is my brother, Alfie, and his partner, Dylan.'

'Oh great, nice to meet you guys, and thank you for helping us,' he said as he shook both of their hands firmly. 'So what kind of business do you two run?'

Alfie looked confused by the odd question. 'I run our family pub that Edward's just mentioned, but Dylan works at Chalk Gap Academy.'

'Yes, I was also there when you were guarding the staff room that day, you probably don't remember me.' Dylan said.

Poor PC Wood looked utterly perplexed. 'Oh, you don't run a business together then? But he said you were partners?' He looked blank for a few seconds until I saw the penny drop as realisation hit him and his expression changed. 'Oh, I see, oh okay... that's amazing, guys! Good for you!'

Alfie and Dylan shared an amused look, before he ushered them off to the Vicarage to guard the crime scene.

I took a deep breath after they left and considered PC Wood. I certainly had my work cut out for me pairing up with him, and I wasn't sure if he was able enough to investigate, if he couldn't even work out that Alfie's partner meant his boyfriend, not his business partner.

To give him credit, looking around I could see he'd done a reasonable job setting up the incident room: making use of the whiteboards, markers and flipchart paper used by the Sunday School to set up what we needed, and setting up the PC and large screen ready for Appleby to video call into us. The bland, neglected, old-fashioned church hall looked purposeful. He'd either used his initiative or (more likely) followed Appleby's instructions, but either way he'd done it well. I was sure that PC Wood was a good police constable, he just wasn't a detective. But neither was I.

10

'Hello mate!' Appleby's voice blasted out through the church hall, the acoustics of the wooden room making it sound hollow and flat. I heard him before I saw him, with his face taking a second to appear, at first inappropriately zoomed in: all I could see was his eyes and right up his nose. I pulled up a chair and small table, sitting myself in front of the screen and using my image in the corner to make sure I would be dead centre of Appleby's view. Seeing myself always makes me anxious, and I straightened up my glasses self-consciously.

By the time I'd finished all that, Appleby had fixed his own screen so I could see him properly. He was holding whatever device he was using at arm's length; I guessed it was his mobile phone. He was wearing an expensive-looking woollen hat and looked freezing, his cheeks bright red but his striking features allowing him to get away with it. I felt a pang of jealousy return; even shivering away in selfie mode, he looked like he'd effortlessly stepped off the set of a Christmas music video. Behind him I could see a bright white background which seemed to be wobbling, and I guessed they'd set up police tents in the fields as far along Chalk Gap Road as they could get.

'Right then, mate,' he started as he looked at me from the screen. 'Let's get going, shall we? Lots to update you on, then you can tell me what you know your end.'

'Don't we need to wait for PC Wood?' I asked.

'Nah, he'll be busy at the crime scene for ages. That's the kind of stuff we need him for, all the donkey work.'

'Oh, alright then.' I felt guilty for the slight sense of relief that I didn't need to work with the over-zealous young officer for now. I already had my own over-enthusiastic sidekick in Noah.

'Yeah, the Crime Scene Examiner will be video calling Wood to do the scene log, and secure all the forensic evidence for when we can get through. On that, still no joy with boat or helicopter, but we've managed to get help at this end from the farmers at Chris George's farm, they're going to fit snow ploughs on their tractors. That should hopefully help us to clear a way through in the next few hours.'

'A few hours?'

'At the least, mate. I'm trying to cover all the official stuff, but I'm relying on your brain to help us crack this one under the circumstances we have. I'll come on to your bit in a minute, let me just finish telling you everything else that's going on.' His voice sounded tired and stressed already. I felt that all the information he was relaying was for his own benefit, to reassure himself, as much as it was for me.

'Where was I, mate?' He continued. 'Right, your village GP is on video call with our Pathologist as we speak. Waiting to hear from them to hopefully get an idea of the time and cause of death.'

'But I can tell you the cause of death, she was -'

'Let's do all that bit officially, mate, so we know where we are. Well I say officially, it won't be official 'til a registered Pathologist confirms it in person, but it will give us an idea. I tell you, it's a bloody nightmare, this snow.' He looked away from the screen as if listening to someone else for a second, and I saw him nod his head to someone off camera.

'What do you want me to do, then?' I was keen to get on.

'Coming to that, Edward. Next, I've got my House to House Team Leader liaising with your mate Kat, to co-ordinate carrying out question-naires of people in the area who might have seen something.'

'How can you do house to house in this?' I didn't even know such a role existed. I could vaguely guess their job description, but the classic style murder mysteries I read didn't cover the police investigation in such detail; they focused on the puzzle: leaving such in depth elements to the grittier police procedural novels.

'Not literally house to house, we're gonna start with everyone stranded around the village square, particularly the people using East Chalk Cliff for sledging. That backs on to the Vicarage and someone there might have seen something.'

'My thoughts exactly.' This was what I'd identified myself earlier, so I should have felt confident in this, but I noticed the drumming of my fingers increase and felt a wave of frustration that Appleby was one step ahead of me. I focused on jotting down what he told me, avoiding looking at the screen.

'Yeah, that will hopefully give us something. Next, we'll talk to all the people in the pub and the volunteer team, the businesses at that end of the village, and if possible any houses we can get to. Kat's got a few reliable people who can help us, mostly your school colleagues. We're on such dodgy ground though, mate, all these jobs are meant to be carried out by constables, not volunteers. We'll have to do all the official stuff later, and if I get my knuckles wrapped for it, fair enough.'

To give Appleby his due, he seemed to be on the ball and doing everything he could at his end under the restrictions he had. I knew how frustrated he would be not being able to get through with his team to do all their usual work. I felt determined to ensure that my part in proceedings would be valuable. Luckily, he seemed to have got to that bit at last.

'Okay, Edward – your turn. Tell me everything you know so far.'

I sat up and started telling him everything I'd seen from the beginning, just as I'd told my friends. As I spoke, I remember starting to relax until I found myself sitting back in my chair, surprising myself with how comfortable I felt sharing my observations.

Appleby spoke after I'd finished. 'Some really good stuff there, well done. Yeah, I agree that the confrontation in the square is a good starting point. Get talking to all the people there for now, and once the Pathologist and Crime Scene Examiner finish their stuff with Doctor Albright and PC Wood, we'll look at what clues we have from the crime scene.'

I imagined this would be my role, and had given some thought to how I went about it. 'We have to do it carefully, some of the people involved are easier to speak to than others.' I thought of poor, grieving Reverend and Jacob Flowers and what they must have been going through.

'Of course, mate. Like I said, nothing formal for now. Just your usual casual poking round and see what you can find out. That'll hopefully give us a good enough idea for when we get through.' He stopped for a moment and I could feel his eyes on me. 'Go on then, what's your plan?'

'I was thinking I'll leave the two Flowers men until last, and hopefully find out what I need from the others in the meantime.'

'Sensible, mate. One of the hardest parts of our job, questioning grieving relatives. I wouldn't expect you to do that unless it comes to it. Hopefully we can pick up that part when we get through.'

'I can talk to Gloria Hernandez easily enough as she's in the volunteer group based at the pub, so I'll probably start with her,' I continued. 'She's fairly chatty anyway so she should be easy to speak to.'

'Sounds good, mate,' Appleby said, but I could tell he was distracted again by someone off screen. 'What about the others?'

'Kimmy and Claire Atkinson have been around this morning too, and their B&B is only just off the square, so I should be able to speak to them okay. My brother's quite friendly with them, so I might get him to help me with that.'

'Good plan.' Appleby's attention was back on me now, and I could tell from his narrowed eyes and focused expression he was trying to listen intently. 'Just remember to replace your brother guarding the crime scene while he does that. I want two people there at all times, so Wood is free to work with my virtual team.'

I liked how thorough Appleby was, and his rounded thinking reminded me of my own. But I couldn't help feeling like one of his junior officers, receiving instructions from their superior.

'Everest Brown I don't know and have never spoken to,' I continued. 'But Noah's struck up conversation with him already, so he can maybe help with that.'

'Just be careful with how you use the young lad,' Appleby commented back, again leaving me feeling put in my place a little.

'Yes, I know,' I snapped back a little too quickly, before hoping he didn't notice. 'He'll be fine with me. Anyway, the one I might struggle to speak to is Pedro Hernandez. I haven't seem him since he stormed away this morning, he might not be in the village centre anymore – he could be snowed in elsewhere in the village.' I had no idea where in the village Pedro lived.

'Ah, hopefully you can get him, mate, he's really important.' Appleby replied. I knew this and cut him off before he could continue.

'Yes, definitely. Especially if I'm not speaking to Reverend Flowers yet. I need Pedro's version of what that was about this morning, and if there's any truth in the Reverend and Cherry thing.' I'd thought about this and wanted him to know I had a plan. 'His restaurant is at this end of the high street near the square, so hopefully I'll be able to get through the snow to try there. I also need to find out where Cherry is and where she's been this morning, as she could be a suspect too.'

'Excellent, Edward. I like your thinking. It's possible this Pedro guy has the wrong end of the stick about the affair, or he has the right end but it's someone else. Although it's not our business if it's not the Vicar. This all sounds good, mate. Keep me posted after each person.'

'Will do,' I said, pleased that my approach seemed to be meeting his approval. 'And while talking to them, I'll keep my ear out for anything else I can about Frances, and anyone else who might have had an issue with her.'

'It's a strange one, mate,' Appleby said in reply as he scratched his nose on screen. 'I mean, who has an issue with the nice, quiet Vicar's wife?'

That's exactly what I'd been thinking too. But I barely knew anything about either Frances or Reverend Flowers outside of their public personas, and anything could have been going on behind closed doors. I suddenly remembered the strange way the Reverend had took all the other ladies in for a cup of tea after the confrontation, but had left his own wife out in the cold. What was that about? I was about to tell Appleby about this, when I heard a phone ring tone off screen and he looked distracted again. 'Hang on a sec, my work phone's going. You're on my personal one so I could keep it free.'

He went off camera and I could hear his muffled voice in the background, but not enough to hear what he was saying. It dawned on me how already this felt so different from my part in the Miss Finch case. Even with my well thought out plans, I still felt like an imposter that didn't belong.

'Okay, we have some news,' Appleby declared as he returned to the screen. He was distracted again though, this time reading through the notes he'd been making as I'd relayed my story earlier. 'What time did you say Frances Flowers left your mum in the pub, about 9.45AM?'

'That's right.' I knew that would become important, so I'd already double checked with Mum and Noah the timeframe of our tea-making, and therefore what time Frances would have left.

'That's what I thought, mate. Your Doctor and the Pathologist have got the time of death to an hour window: somewhere between 9.30 and 10.30, but definitely no later than 10.30. Therefore, she was killed within 45 minutes of leaving you guys at the pub.'

11

'How exciting! All we have to do is track Frances Flowers' movements in that 45 minutes and we'll solve the case.'

I'd finished the video call with Appleby and immediately jumped on hearing Noah's voice, who it turned out had been sat at the back of the church hall the whole time.

'Noah, what are you doing here?' I questioned as I turned to him.

'I thought that I need to be kept in the loop, but I knew the DI wouldn't let me in on police business. So I stayed silent the whole time, even you didn't know I was there,' he said proudly as he grinned at me. 'Aren't you impressed?'

I considered him for a moment as he stood beaming at me. This case was becoming more puzzling by the minute, and when you have a puzzle to solve, Noah's unique insight is sometimes just what you need.

'Yes I am, very much,' I said warmly, deciding not to tell him off for sneaking in and listening. 'So, what do you think of what you heard?'

I gestured him to come and sit down as I spoke, and he came hurtling over to join me at the table. His eyes lit up when he saw all the various stationery – flipchart paper, markers, highlighters, post-its – waiting to be used.

'I think it's really sad for poor Frances Flowers.'

'Really?' I don't know quite what I expected his answer to be – likely something about narrowing the suspects down, or some kind of murder mystery plot twist he was expecting – but it wasn't that.

He plonked himself down on the seat and looked straight at me. 'I was just thinking about it. I'm excited to investigate who did it, but it's really sad too. She was a nice lady and we were making a cup of tea for her. But less than an hour later, she was dead.' He stopped speaking and I noticed he looked quite sombre. All of a sudden though, he picked up a marker pen and pulled the flipchart paper towards him. 'Shall we work out who killed her then? I'm looking forward to another puzzle to solve.'

I stopped myself shaking my head as I watched him write Frances' name down in the centre of the paper. Perhaps the bigger puzzle to solve was how Noah's mind worked. Thinking of the murder victim as a real person, even one he felt sorry for, was huge progress for him. But then he switched that part of his brain back off and went immediately back into storybook detective mode.

Maybe I needed to be more like him. I too felt sad for Frances, but the difference was it was weighing on my mind; it was unsettling me. The revelation that she'd left our pub and was killed within 45 minutes felt too close to home; it was almost literally on our doorstep. Frances was a pleasant but quiet and meek lady, who had surely done little harm to anyone and was one of the last people I'd expect to be brutally murdered.

But she had, and it was time to find out why.

12

'You don't need to look any further, Pedro did it.'

Gloria Hernandez hadn't wasted any time naming her ex-husband as the number one suspect, pronouncing him guilty as soon as we found her in the village square.

I was surprised to see her back in her market hut for *Sweets for your Sweet*, the only trader now out on the winter market except for Everest Brown at *Burger She Wrote*. I could understand Everest, as a stranger with no emotional attachment to Frances Flowers (though I needed to find out his connection to the Reverend), carrying on with business as usual – although he maybe should have been helping clear snow instead – after the body had been discovered only a few feet from the market. But Gloria was the Flowers' best friend and here she was trying to sell Christmas candy canes like nothing was wrong. More so, she'd roped me and Noah into helping her, in exchange for helping us to solve her close friend's murder (she'd seen straight through my excuse to speak to her and knew I was investigating – probably thanks to Mum's announcement in the pub).

'You might as well make yourselves useful if you want any more information out of me,' she'd said once she'd finished slandering her ex-husband, obviously expecting payment in labour to slander him in more detail.

The price of 'information' was lugging several boxes of sweets through the deep snow, from her storage cupboard in the church hall (another perk), across the square to her hut. I'd even tried to persuade her to come sit down in the investigation room while we were in the same building, but she was having none of it. I was attempting to wade through knee high snow, while trying to focus on carrying three large boxes of various sweets, and listen to Gloria (who wasn't actually carrying anything) at the same time.

'As if the Vicar would go anywhere near that little jezebel,' she was saying as she trotted along in front of us, making the trek through the snow look easy.

'You don't think it's true then?' Noah's voice enquired from behind a tower of boxes.

Gloria stopped dead in front of us and turned around. I got a whiff of her strong, feminine perfume in the cold air. 'Of course it isn't true.' She snapped as she stared out Noah.

'Why would Pedro say that?' Noah asked in his usual innocent tone.

'Because he's an idiot,' she said dismissively as she brushed the falling snow off her shoulders.

'So, Cherry McDonald isn't having an affair?' Noah continued. I let out a frustrated sigh; I'd come on to how Cherry related to everything (including her current whereabouts), but I wanted to shift the conversation back to the victim, Frances.

'Of course she's having an affair!' Gloria said sharply, her voice cutting through the ice cold. 'My moron ex-husband just got the wrong guy, that's all. It could be anyone. That's what happens when you take up with a trollop more than half your age.'

Thankfully, we'd arrived back at the market and I was relieved to put the boxes of sweets down in the back of the hut. I was worried about running out of time with Gloria - who hadn't told us much beyond her own biased opinion so far – and I decided to strike. 'Gloria, is there anything concrete you can tell us about Frances' death that might help us? Did you see her again after the confrontation in the square, for example?'

We stepped back out of the hut without her replying to me, and then she glanced at her watch before gesturing over to the pub. 'Just gone 1 o'clock, not too early for the first glass of wine of the day. Let's go have a drink and I'll see what I can remember. It's on you, by the way.'

13

I felt guilty stood at the bar waiting, as I watched Dad pour a large red wine for Gloria. I'd already spent nearly half an hour carrying boxes, and now I was back in the pub buying her a drink. I'd expected my investigations to be more active and more fruitful than this; I was worried I was wasting time.

'So all she's talked about so far is how she thinks Pedro did it?' Dad asked as he served me.

'That's all. Oh and how Cherry was definitely having an affair with someone, but not Reverend Flowers,' I replied as I drummed my fingers on the bar.

'She's bound to say that, on both counts!' Dad remarked. 'Everyone round here knows she hates Pedro after he took up with young Cherry. She's made enough song and dance about it over the last year or so!'

I only had a vague recollection of all of this, and realised that I didn't actually know the timeframe of the Fernandez' split and Pedro's affair with Cherry. I wish I'd paid more attention to Mum's gossip the dozens of times she'd told me this story.

'Is that when Gloria and Pedro broke up, a year or so ago?' I asked Dad.

'It must be about that, yes,' Dad replied as he poured a draft lemonade for Noah. 'Actually, I remember exactly when it was. There was a big scandal about Gloria finding out about Pedro and Cherry on Christmas Day, terrible to-do it was. She kicked him out on the day. So yep, that was a year and a bit ago.'

Of course. I remembered the Christmas Day fiasco as soon as Dad mentioned it. It was a drama worthy of a soap opera festive episode. And I realised that it wasn't as long ago as I thought. No wonder Gloria hated her ex-husband. But those raw emotions made her bias very real; I made a mental note to take anything related to Pedro with a bigger pinch of salt than I was already.

'I need to find out what I can from her about Frances, but she just keeps going on about Pedro,' I complained to Dad as he took my alcoholic ginger beer from the fridge. 'She knows exactly what she's doing in making me wait too, she thinks it's a game.'

'Oh yes, she'll run rings round you, that one.'

'But Dad, her so called best friend is dead. She knows I'm helping to investigate it. Why would she mess me around?'

'Firstly,' my dad said as he put the three drinks onto a tray, 'what makes you think they're best friends? Edward, what you have to remember about certain women round here...' He stopped and looked cautiously over his shoulder before he continued; presumably Mum was one of these 'certain women' and he didn't want her over-hearing him. 'Certain women round here act like they're best friends but they're not. Frenemies, I think they call it. Your mum, for example, is nice as pie to Gloria every time she's in the pub, but she'd shed as few tears as she did for Miss Finch if Gloria was the one who died.'

Ridiculous gender stereotyping aside, he had a point. I'd seen Mum make nice with dozens of women in the village, only to then say different once they'd left the pub. That probably says more about my mum than anything, but the point was just because Gloria *appeared* to be Frances' friend, it didn't mean she was.

I mean, she could be your killer,' Dad continued. 'Maybe she's after the Vicar and got Frances out of the way.'

The ridiculousness of this floated into my mind for a second, before I dismissed it. It could be true. The fact was, Frances had been killed, likely by someone she knew well, and it could be for any reason. I had to piece together the different accounts from the various people close to her, but I knew from painful previous experience not to trust anyone.

I'd not replied to Dad, and without realising it I'd zoned out and was staring into space. I was brought back when I felt Dad's hand on mine on the bar.

'Son,' he started quietly. 'You already solved one murder when no one else could. You can do this. I believe in you.' He then withdrew his hand, and went back to washing glasses as if he hadn't said anything.

I thanked him and returned to the table with a renewed determination to get something useful out of Gloria. I got there to find her in full monologue mode about Pedro's certain guilt, with Noah typing away hurriedly into his phone trying to keep up.

'Okay Gloria,' I said with as much confidence as I could muster as I put the drinks down on the table. 'We know your theories about Pedro, but let's move on. I want to talk about Frances, specifically. Starting with if you saw her alive again after the confrontation in the square.'

She looked shocked. To be fair, I'd shocked myself. I could feel my heart racing as I took my seat, and the words I'd just said felt like they were someone else's.

She narrowed her eyes and considered me carefully. 'Edward, no offence, sweetheart, but I don't have to tell you anything. I mean, you're nobody.'

I felt the sting of those last two words, but I had

to push through. 'Maybe, but I thought you'd rather clear things up with me now, rather than go through it with the police when they get here.'

She glared at me again, then her whole demeanour changed and she started laughing. 'Edward, course I'll talk to you, I'm sorry. Thanks for the drink, by the way. Cheers.' She picked up her wine glass and did an imaginary toasting gesture before she took a sip. I noticed the strong smell of her perfume again.

'You're welcome. And thank you,' I said in reply as I picked up my drink and made the same gesture. I glanced at Noah who was still hurriedly typing, presumably behind in noting down her speech about Pedro.

'I'm not heartless, you know,' she said. 'I just act up sometimes, especially when I've had a shock. I mean, my good friend has been murdered and I want Ped-, I mean I want whoever did this caught. Now, what do you want to know?'

I took a moment to think about my next move with this whirlwind of a woman. I asked my question for the third time this morning. 'Did you see Frances after the incident at the market?'

She took a sip of her wine and pulled a face. 'Tell your family they really need to get a better house red.'

I wondered if she was going to say anymore or if she was still playing games, but then she spoke again. 'Yes, yes I did, as it happens. Reverend Flowers took me, Kimmy and Claire into the Vicarage for a cup of tea. He sat us down in the living room, then went off to the kitchen to make the drinks. About ten minutes later, he came back with the tea. But just as he was handing the cups out, Frances appeared at the living room door looking like a ghost.' She stopped and I could tell she'd realised her ill choice of description, but she didn't correct herself.

'Then what happened?' Noah asked, speaking for the first time in a while, now up to date with his previous notes and fingers on his phone at the ready for a set of new ones.

'She asked Reverend Flowers if she could speak to him in private, but he told her it would have to wait until we'd all left.'

This was interesting. It also fitted into how Flowers invited all the ladies back for tea 'to get over the shock' of the confrontation, but excluded his own wife, who looked most shocked of all. He seemed to be actively avoiding her after Pedro's accusation; did this mean it was true?

I decided to see what Gloria thought of this. 'Why do you think the Reverend was avoiding speaking to her, if he wasn't having an affair?'

'I guess you don't know Reverend Flowers very well,' she sneered. 'He's a very private man and he didn't want a scene. He was embarrassed enough as it was, he didn't want to add to it by having a public argument with his wife.'

'But she asked to speak to him in private,' Noah pointed out, earning himself a deathly look from Gloria.

'Yes, but it doesn't take a genius to work out what about. He just wanted to get back to normal and act like it hadn't happened.' She tutted and rolled her eyes, but I wasn't sure who exactly in regard to: Noah, Reverend Flowers or Frances. I was still fairly new to questioning people about a murder, but she was certainly more difficult to read than anyone I'd questioned before.

'He didn't discuss the incident with you all then?' I asked.

'Not directly. He just kept checking we were okay, apologising for the upset, then went off to make tea. But we could tell he was unhappy.' She paused and I could see she was considering what she would say next. 'Reverend Flowers is very proud, and he doesn't like situations he's not in control of.'

'Reverend Flowers... likes to be in control...' Noah murmured aloud to himself as he frantically typed away. 'So he didn't go and speak to Mrs Flowers then?'

'He did, actually. She insisted that it was important and she wasn't moving without him coming with her. Which was quite out of character for her.'

On the surface, it really was. But public and private lives are two very different things, often even to our close friends and family. We knew nothing of France's character or the Flowers' marriage: only other people's interpretations of it. What I wanted to do to finish this conversation was establish some facts.

'Did they come back to join you after they spoke privately?' I asked.

'No, we waited about fifteen minutes then we decided it was best to leave them to it. So we left.'

'We – that's you, Kimmy and Claire?'

'Yes, officer,' she remarked back. Maybe I was laying it on thick but I wanted to find out what I needed to, and she hadn't been the easiest person to speak to.

'Did you overhear any of their conversation before you left?' I only vaguely remembered the layout of the Vicarage – I'd been in a few times as a child when the old Vicar used to live there – but I knew it wasn't very big inside, so there was a chance the conversation didn't stay completely private.

'Edward, what do you take me for?' She said in mock innocence, putting her hand on her chest. 'No we didn't overhear anything. We could hear their voices but that's it. Kimmy and Claire will tell you the same. If Reverend Flowers wanted the conversation to stay private, it would have stayed private.'

'And did you go out the front or the back of the Vicarage?'

'The front.' Her face changed again as she rounded on me. 'Wait, the back was where she was found, wasn't it? I hope you're not suggesting the Reverend was out there murdering his wife while we sat in his front room drinking tea.'

I assured her I wasn't thinking that, but was I? The Vicar would seem to be the prime suspect, with a motive and opportunity. Or it could have been a marital dispute gone wrong; it wasn't too far fetched. There could have been a history of domestic violence in the marriage and today things got out of hand. I was starting to feel out of my depth again, and secretly hoped that Appleby would make his way through the snow and take over the investigation.

I tried to breathe and think things through, before I let Gloria Hernandez on her way. On sheer logistics, Reverend Flowers was looking like a possibility; he was on the scene at the time, having a private conversation with his wife shortly before the murder. Pedro Hernandez or Cherry McDonald (wherever she was) probably wouldn't have time to wade through the snow to get to the Vicarage, Jacob Flowers and Everest Brown were both on the market (I needed to check if they were there the whole time), and the three women had left together. But this was about twenty-five minutes into the forty-five minute window; did they stay together? If Gloria left the Atkinsons once she left the Vicarage, she still would have had time to re-turn to kill Frances.

I had my next question. 'Did you three go your separate ways once you left the Vicarage?'

'Actually, not quite. Claire went back to the B&B to check on their guests, but Kimmy stayed with me to see how we could help elsewhere. She was with me another half hour at least.'

That would put the two of them out of the frame if Kimmy backed this up later. Either that or co-murderers. 'Where did you go, into the pub to Kat?'

'Oh no, I don't need that Head Teacher woman allocating jobs to me. We had a wander round the square and around the bottom of each cliff, we were mainly seeing if anyone needed any sweets to cheer them up.'

A sales drive for her sweet shop, then. After the last half hour spent with Gloria, I wasn't particu-larly surprised to hear this. I thanked her and she went on her way, reminding me one more time to make sure the police look at her ex-husband as a suspect.

14

Thankfully, my experience speaking to Kimmy and Claire Atkinson couldn't have been more different from my one with Gloria. Alfie, being friends with them (which was actually news to me), had managed to arrange for the two of us to go and see them at the B&B. He'd swapped out his crime scene duty with Noah for half an hour, and we were due for early afternoon tea with the couple. I wondered if my bladder would cope with all the refreshments involved in this investigation so far.

Their B&B was just off the square on the corner of the high street, so we only had a couple of minutes trudge through the snow to get there. It was still falling rapidly and although the half dozen or so volunteers had manage to clear the first few yards of road, I could see that it wouldn't be too long until it was covered again. I wondered if the police were any closer to finding a way through. I hadn't heard from DI Appleby or PC Wood since before I spoke to Gloria, and I resolved to make contact once I'd finished with Kimmy and Claire. My feet were painfully cold already and I was keen to get into the warmth of the B&B.

On the way over, I asked Alfie how his friendship with Kimmy and Claire had come about. I was a little surprised to hear about it, as it seemed a little stereotypical for the two gay couples in our village to suddenly be friends (especially as my brother and Dylan hadn't even been a couple that long), and Alfie wasn't stereotypically gay (though I knew Dylan had been trying to convert him to *Rupaul's Drag Race*) and had always shied away from the gay scene, even with us having Brighton down the road.

'They're a lovely couple, but yeah, it was a strange one. It was a few months ago, a couple of weeks after me and Dylan had gone public. I noticed they'd suddenly started coming in the pub for a drink a few times, always making small talk with me when they got served. Well, Kimmy more so. She's the more outgoing one of the two, you'll see when you meet her.'

This tied in with what I knew of her already and I told him so before he continued.

'Anyway, this one evening, Dylan was sat at the bar keeping me company when they came in. Instead of going to sit down like they had been doing, they asked if they could join us at the bar. Dylan and Kimmy especially got on really well, they ended up getting drunk together. Next thing I knew, we'd been asked round to theirs for dinner that weekend.'

'How did you feel about that?' Alfie had never been a big socialiser (despite running a pub) and had only started spending time with our group of friends since Dylan's arrival.

'I wasn't keen at first, I thought Dylan would have more in common with them than I do. But I enjoyed it actually, we've done it a few more times since. We love seeing you guys, but it's nice to have another couple to spend time with, and I can talk about business stuff with them as well.' Of course. The B&B and pub were both at the heart of Chalk Gap hospitality, so it made sense for their respective proprietors to support each other. Although I wondered Mum's views on this.

'But you said it was a strange one? Do you think they were deliberately trying to befriend you guys? And that's why they were going in the pub all of a sudden?'

He laughed and turned to face me as we reached the gate of the B&B. 'Oh Edward, I love the way your mind works. Always trying to tie up every loose end and tick every box. No wonder you keep getting roped into these murder cases.'

I smiled back at him. 'You thought the same too though, I could tell by the way you told me.'

'Yep, yes I did. It did seem like they were trying to befriend us especially, but it's turned out well in the end.' He shivered through the fashionable but light jacket he wore, folding his arms and rubbing his shoulders to keep warm.

'You don't think either of them are potential murderers then?'

He laughed again. 'Not as far as I know! Though I suppose we've all learned that you never know.' His tone was more serious now as his teeth chattered in the cold. 'They're really nice ladies, but I know you're gonna tell me it has to be someone. I suppose everyone under suspicion is nice.'

I thought of my dreadful half hour or so with Gloria, and also what I'd seen and heard about Reverend Flowers. 'Not necessarily.'

'Edward, why is this happening in our village again?' There was anger in his voice now and I could see his gloved hands clenching into fists. 'Frances Flowers wouldn't hurt a fly, and yet she's been murdered on our doorstep. I just don't understand it. We've grown up here and nothing has barely happened in all that time. What's happening to our quiet little Chalk Gap?'

I didn't know it as we had that conversation, but Frances' murder was only the half of it.

15

'Are you sure you don't want another cupcake, Edward?'

'No, thank you, Kimmy, I honestly couldn't eat anything else.' It was true. Kimmy and Claire had pulled out all the stops for our early afternoon tea, which we hadn't asked for and I didn't even really have time for. But it was impressive. Especially impressive when we'd arranged our visit in less than an hour. The cynical part of me thought of Frances Flowers lying dead and wondered what other plans they could pull off in the same time-frame.

I'd learned two things about Kimmy and Claire fairly early into us arriving: that they were very happy together, and that they knew how to run a successful business. The B&B was a large cottage which they'd converted into a guest house, and the building itself had all the charms of rural village life. I'm not very good at describing interior design (apart from bookshelves), as it's not something that really takes my interest, but the rustic wooden floors and pastel colours of the walls and furnishings made it seem homely and cared for; I could see why tourists loved it (Mum had previously read out some of their Trip Advisor reviews to me, when she was wondering why they scored higher than the pub).

But the real appeal of the B&B was the two people who ran and lived in it. They frequently referred to it as 'our home' and it was clear they loved it and each other. They frequently finished each other's sentences, agreed with each other's points and backed each other up.

They'd made the afternoon tea together, as they did every day for their guests, and I could see every effort had been made in preparing our feast: delicious sandwiches with homemade bread; a range of mouth-watering meats and cheeses from a deli in Eastbourne (presumably before the snow storm but tasting as fresh as if bought that day); a selection of homemade jams and marmalades; freshly baked scones and beautiful, bright hand-decorated cupcakes.

As I'd finished the little taste of heaven that was my last cupcake, I remember thinking that I'd be heartbroken if either of these two ended up being the murderer. I was glad that it was Alfie who was here with me, as I knew Noah would be trying (and failing) to whisper in my ear not to trust the nicest suspects, and repeating the Poirot quote where he said 'every murderer is probably somebody's old friend.'

The first half hour passed with general chit-chat and pleasantries, with Frances' death only being mentioned in a general way about how shocking it was. But I knew I had a purpose in being there, and I had to get to it. I didn't have to wait long after we'd eaten, however, as Claire beat me to it.

'So, Edward, it's really nice to have you over, but should we talk about what you want to know from us? We know that's why you're here.'

To be fair, she said it in a friendly enough way and smiled gently as she spoke, but the dismay on my face must have shown. 'Why I'm here?'

'Yes, everyone knows you're helping the police until they can get through the snow,' Kimmy added as she helped herself to another cupcake. 'We were pleased when Alfie called us to bring you round, we want to help.'

Alfie had the good grace to look embarrassed at being caught out but Claire reassured him. 'Honestly, don't worry. We've heard all about Edward's detective work and we're glad he's looking into it. We want Frances' killer found.' That pronoun 'we' had now been used multiple times in about 30 seconds, and I wondered where the 'we' ended and how much they were two individuals.

'Yes, we'll tell you everything you want to know,' Kimmy added, through a mouthful of cupcake.

'Thank you both, I just want to establish whatever facts I can until the police get here. You won't know yet, but they've confirmed that it's a 45 minute window between Frances leaving Mum at the pub and Reverend Flowers finding the body.'

A few seconds after I said that last word, I heard a long, low pitched wail and it took me a few seconds to realise that Kimmy had started crying.

Claire was straight to her feet and went behind Kimmy's chair, cradling her gently as she sobbed. 'It's okay, baby, it's okay,' she whispered in soothing tones.

'I'm sorry,' Kimmy said through sniffles as she wiped her eyes. 'It's just when you said "body," it really got to me.

'It's understandable,' Alfie said, looking a little embarrassed once again.

'I'm sorry,' I muttered at pretty much the same time, my words overlapping with my brother's. From Gloria Hernandez' antics to this, I realised the difference from my last investigation. Even if it was difficult questioning my friends and colleagues last time, at least I had an idea of how they would act while we spoke. This time round, I had no clue how they'd behave because I didn't really know the suspects, which made them unpredictable. I hated unpredictable.

'It's not your fault, Edward,' Claire said as she continued to comfort her wife. 'It's just such a huge shock. I know there was that business with the Head Teacher last year, but things like this don't happen to people like us. Who could want Frances dead?'

'Exactly,' I said firmly, my confidence coming back. 'That's all I want to know too. Just whatever you can tell me about Frances. Talk me through the incident this morning, and help me establish where everyone was in that 45 minutes when she was killed. Does that sound alright?'

'Yes, of course, anything you need,' Claire said as she returned to her seat. Kimmy made a sniffle noise again, and continued to wipe her eyes with her jumper sleeve.

'Actually, I will have another of those cupcakes,' I said as I reached across the table. 'They're delicious.'

I'd hoped this would cheer Kimmy up and it seemed to work. 'Thank you, Edward, we made them together this morning.' She paused for a second and reached for another cupcake herself. 'I'm sorry about getting upset. I just can't believe someone murdered Frances. She was the nicest... the nicest of all of them.'

'What do you mean, all of them?' Alfie asked before I could.

'Nothing,' Claire intercepted quickly. 'She just means the nicest of all the people we know.' I considered the way Kimmy said "all of them" and thought of the way they'd made a play to be friends with my brother and Dylan. Was it because they were trying to get out of Reverend Flowers' close-knit friend group? I kept quiet for the time being, but this was something to keep my eye on.

'Not to worry,' I said as brightly as I could. 'Do you just want to tell me about this morning after the confrontation in the square?'

Kimmy was about to speak, but Claire cut in and started to tell the story instead. Her account of what happened inside the vicarage matched Gloria's completely, which I'd guessed it would; Gloria seemed too smart to say something that couldn't be backed up by others.

'When you decided to leave and give them privacy, that was out the main front door to the vicarage?'

'Oh I wish we'd gone out of the back door,' Kimmy wailed. 'We might have prevented it.'

'The front door, yes,' Claire confirmed with a nod of her head and a smile. 'Kimmy's right. I wish we'd checked on them before we left.'

I'd told them I wanted to know more about Frances and this was my chance. 'Have you seen them argue like that before?'

They both looked at each other, as if waiting for the other one to answer. 'Not really,' Claire finally answered before both looked down, avoiding all eye contact.

There was obviously much more to this. As I was thinking how to approach this next, Alfie spoke up. 'Look, I know this is difficult and a little awkward to talk about.' He looked at me and gave a small smile. 'But you have to trust my brother. You're not betraying anyone if you just tell us the truth about the Flowers and what you know. Even something small might be important.'

The couple met each other's eyes again, this time nodding to each other. 'The thing is,' Claire started. 'The thing is, that lately we've been a bit uncomfortable with -'

'We hate them all!' Kimmy blurted out before putting her hands over her mouth in a cartoon way.

'We don't hate anyone,' Claire clarified, sounding panicked. 'And we did like Frances, very much, she was a lovely lady and a good friend of ours.'

'Why don't you tell us about it?' Alfie said gently. 'What have you been uncomfortable with?'

There was a moment's silence, when all I could hear was the sound of Kimmy nervously eating the last bite of her cupcake. Until Claire spoke again.

'We've been friends with that group for a couple of years or so now, since we moved to the village. At first it was nice, we were all in couples: me and Kimmy, Gloria and Pedro, the Reverend and Frances.' It occurred to me that everyone always called him the Reverend or Reverend Flowers, and never Allan – not even his close friends.

'I liked those days,' Kimmy said sadly. 'We'd just moved from Brighton and it was so lovely to make friends in the village.'

'What changed?' Alfie asked. I knew what their first answer would be.

'Gloria and Pedro splitting up was the first issue. It was such a bitter break-up and it cut through our friendship group,' Claire said.

'We felt like we were back at school,' Kimmy added, having stopped crying now. 'Having to take sides like that. We tried to stay friends with Pedro, but Gloria was having none of it, and Reverend Flowers agreed. As soon as he said that, it was decision made.'

'And I know what Pedro did to Gloria was awful, cheating like that. But he didn't do it to us, and -'

'We prefer Pedro to Gloria anyway!' Kimmy cut in, interrupting her wife.

'You've got to stop doing that, baby,' Claire said back to her, but it was with warmth and they both laughed. 'Let's just say that we don't quite enjoy the friendship group as much as we used to.'

I'm glad I wasn't the only one who didn't exactly take to Gloria. 'Why did you prefer Pedro?'

'He's just very kind and very funny,' Kimmy replied. 'We got on well with him.'

'And you don't with Gloria?' I probably knew the answer to that already. I could see from both of these meetings today that they were completely different women from Gloria. But they were too polite to say that outright.

'She can be a nice lady,' Claire explained. 'But the break-up hit her hard and she's not really been the same since.'

'In what way?' I asked. I hoped I'd remember all these comments. I needed Noah here to take notes as I knew he'd get away with it; it seemed rude me or Alfie doing it.

'She can be quite bitchy.' Kimmy blurted out quickly before covering her mouth again, with only one hand this time. 'I'm sorry, I shouldn't say that.'

I couldn't stop myself from grinning. 'It's okay, I spent an hour with her before I came here.'

'See, he knows what she's like then!' Kimmy directed her words to her wife, who reached out and put her hand on her shoulder.

'As you've probably seen for yourself, Gloria is a big character,' Claire said. 'Which means she can be quite bossy sometimes.'

'We're not allowed to be friends with Pedro!'

Claire rubbed Kimmy's shoulder to comfort her. 'She's right. Reverend Flowers had a word with Pedro and told him it was best if he stopped socialising with everyone. But we just took that to mean the whole group when Gloria was there, so we still met up with him a few times.'

Alfie asked the question this time; I'd already guessed the answer. 'And Gloria found out and didn't like it?'

'You know what this town is like, you can't go to the toilet without everyone knowing,' Kimmy said.

'It's interesting, though, it wasn't *just* Gloria who told us off,' Claire said. Again, I guessed where this was going, and I could tell by Claire's tone she wanted to move the conversation on to this topic. 'Reverend Flowers and Gloria both sat us down together to speak to us. We could tell that Gloria wanted to read us the riot act, but the Reverend did most of the talking in his usual calm, measured way: explaining how we must stick together as a group of friends and not betray the trust of *our dear friend Gloria.*'

'Making it clear, without saying the actual words, that it was either Pedro or them,' Kimmy added.

'I would have chosen Pedro,' my brother remarked.

'It wasn't as easy as that, I'm afraid.' Claire's reply didn't surprise me; I was starting to realise the level of influence Reverend Flowers had. 'It would be very difficult for us not to be friends with Reverend Flowers.'

'In what ways?' Alfie asked. I had an idea what ways. With the influence the local Vicar had in a tiny village like ours, I expected that he could make or break small business holders like Kimmy and Claire. Luckily for Mum, who prided herself in not being one of 'the Vicar's cronies,' the Chalk had been long-standing as the only pub in the village for so long, that the Vicar's machinations probably couldn't have much effect on it.

'We love our B&B so much, we couldn't bear to lose it,' Kimmy whined, confirming the answer I expected without actually answering it directly.

'Surely you weren't just friends with the Reverend because of the influence he had?' Alfie asked.

The room went quiet and I could tell they were both thinking of how to answer this. 'No, and it isn't fair of us to suggest that,' Claire finally said. 'Reverend Flowers is, I think, ultimately a good man. He's very kind, does wonders for the community and has helped us out a great deal over the years.'

If this was the clearly more naïve Kimmy speaking, I might have doubted this, but Claire's softly spoken but assertive words seemed honest and astute. 'What more can you tell us about him as a person, then?' I prompted.

'He cares about this village and all of his parish so much, and he would do anything to help anyone in need. And he loves all of us close to him,' she continued.

There was a 'but' coming, I could tell, but I wasn't sure if it would come without prompting. 'But?'

'He likes to keep his family and close friends very close to him, and be very involved in all of our lives, but...' I could tell she was choosing her words carefully as she looked at Kimmy. 'But sometimes that can be a little over-bearing.'

Reverend Flowers' controlling tendencies were evident, but I needed to find out if it was significant where it mattered. 'Do you mind if I ask, what was the Reverend's relationship with his wife like? Do you think they were happy together?'

The two went quiet again and looked at each other. I really admired their loyalty to him, even though the friendship was obviously rocky.

'I'd say they seemed happier when we first met them,' Kimmy answered this time.

'Yes, the trouble they've had with Jacob in the last year or so hasn't helped,' Claire added.

This was intriguing. I'd felt like Jacob was a factor in this case, and I'd already seen his angry, unpredictable ways. 'How so?'

'He just really started going off the rails,' Claire replied.

'Refusing to go to lessons at the sixth form, angry all the time, really into this goth stuff. But it all got worse when he got obsessed with a girl in his class. He was infatuated with her, he almost got kicked out of school over it,' Kimmy explained. 'Gloria sweet talked Pedro into giving him a job at the restaurant to try and distract him, help mature him a bit. That was going well and he really liked it there, but as you saw this morning, he's been fired from there now.'

And the poor teenager had also just lost his Mum, which wasn't going to help his mental health at all. 'What about the Reverend and Frances specifically? Was she always so quiet around you all?'

'Yes, she was,' Kimmy said.

'She never used to be, actually,' Claire clarified. 'But the last year or so we've noticed the difference.'

'Is she quieter when she's around her husband?' I asked.

'We never really saw her without her husband.'

We'd been talking for a long time and I still had to see the Vicar himself, Jacob, Pedro and Everest, as well as check in with Appleby and see if we had any update on them getting through the snow. I was getting a good idea of the Flowers' marriage as I thought of my last few questions.

'Do you mind if I ask, what do you think of Pedro's accusation? Do you think Reverend Flowers and Cherry are having an affair?'

The couple both looked at each other yet again. They'd clearly not decided beforehand exactly how much they were going to disclose. 'We should tell them what we think,' Kimmy said to her wife.

'Yes, I think you're right,' Claire replied, taking her hand. 'You see, Edward, yes we do. We're pretty sure that, yes, Reverend Flowers is having an affair with Cherry. But we know something else too, that no one else does. Pedro and Cherry actually got married earlier this year. They're husband and wife.'

16

'Wow, that's a crazy group of friends, Edward.'

Alfie and I were outside the B&B, having just left. We were faced with almost waist high snow now, as it had continued to fall in full force during our early afternoon tea. Claire had lent us both a shovel each to help us get back across to the pub. I could see various volunteers still shovelling away on the main high street road, but they looked no further on than they were an hour ago. The village was in crisis, even without the murder, and I hoped that our older and more vulnerable residents were safe, and had everything they needed with help from all the volunteers.

But my focus had to be the murder. I needed to contact Appleby to update each other, but it was helpful for now to discuss the latest turn of events with my brother while we started to shovel our way home.

'It's not looking good for the Reverend, is it?' He remarked as we tried to dig our way through the wall of snow.

It wasn't. I was starting to think we wouldn't learn much more than supposition from Kimmy and Claire, but their revelations at the end were very interesting indeed. It turned out that they'd secretly remained friends with Pedro, and this was the source of most of their information.

Pedro had married Cherry in the summer in secret, in a small ceremony at Eastbourne town hall with Kimmy and Claire as witnesses. Getting a divorce from Gloria had been easy; neither of them had much money to settle, but Pedro's agreement to cite the affair in the divorce and sign over half the restaurant (with Gloria silent partner) made her sign things quickly and quietly.

It had seemed that Pedro and Cherry were very much in love before the wedding. Claire and Kimmy were surprised to see how well they got on; Cherry seemed to genuinely care about Pedro, despite being only in her early twenties and therefore half his age. They knew that people round the village thought she must be a gold-digger ('people' such as Mum), but Pedro was pretty much broke outside of his struggling restaurant, and Cherry herself apparently came from a wealthy family.

However, in the last couple of months, Pedro had taken to coming over to the B&B alone, full of suspicions that Cherry was having an affair: she was out a lot, had become distant and was always on her phone. He followed her one afternoon last week when she claimed to be going shopping in Eastbourne, and saw her go into the Vicarage. Frances Flowers was in the flower shop and therefore not at home, so he soon concluded that Reverend Flowers was the mystery man.

Claire and Kimmy agreed to do some digging of their own, and when Kimmy – in her ever so diplomatic way – deliberately mentioned Cherry's name, Reverend Flowers became very flustered and went red in the face. This had been enough for the three of them to conclude that Flowers and Cherry were guilty.

'Claire and Kimmy don't miss a thing, do they?' Alfie said as he laughed, casting a pile of snow aside. 'They'll give you and Noah a run for your money as the next crime-solving duo. Don't tell him, he'll have the four of you teaming up.'

Joking aside, they had provided us with a very important lead, potentially allowing us to eliminate a suspect. I must admit that I'd considered Pedro a possible suspect after I saw how angry he was on the square, especially now that I knew that the affair rumours seemed to be true, and that the stakes were much higher than I thought in that he was actually married to Cherry. He could have confronted Reverend Flowers, found Frances instead and it had gone horribly wrong.

So I was surprised when Claire revealed that Pedro had been with her for the remainder of the 45 minute window of Frances' murder. As I already knew, Claire, Kimmy and Gloria left the Vicarage when the Flowers' were still arguing, and

Kimmy had been roped into helping Gloria sell her sweets round the square. Claire had returned to the B&B to find a distraught Pedro sat on her doorstep, so she invited him in for tea and he stayed there for over an hour.

Kimmy and Claire also noted that it was unlikely to be Cherry herself who'd murdered her alleged love rival, as Pedro had kicked her out the night before, before the snow started, and he'd watched her leave. He'd got blind drunk afterwards and passed out, and come to confront Reverend Flowers when he woke up in the morning.

Therefore, with Kimmy and Gloria, and Claire and Pedro, giving each other alibis for the murder timeframe, that only left Reverend Flowers, Jacob Flowers (and I didn't see why he'd kill his own mum), Everest Brown (who I'd forgot to ask Claire and Kimmy about) or persons unknown. My brother was right, that it wasn't looking good for the Reverend (not to mention Mum with her earlier 'it's always the husband' comment), but I knew enough about murder – even fictional murder – to not go with the obvious conclusion just yet.

We were digging across the square when I heard a voice calling my name behind us. 'Edward! Excuse me, Edward, my friend!'

I turned to see Pedro calling us. He was further down the high street, walking towards us via the road itself rather than the pavement, using the path that had already been cleared to move faster than he would through the snow. 'My friend, Edward, wait for me – I need to speak to you!'

For some reason - it might have been the quiet, subdued atmosphere caused by the snow – his accent sounded much thicker than I'd noticed it this morning. Keeping myself to myself as I do, Pedro was another villager I knew by sight to say hello to, with details added from Mum's gossip. Thus, I'd not had many conversations with the man and hadn't heard him speak much before. Patrick, who is also Spanish, has lived in England most of his life and doesn't have a noticeable accent, but Pedro certainly did.

We stopped and waited as he caught up to us, and as he stumbled along I noticed his appearance for the first time. He appeared to be wearing overhead wireless headphones in place of ear-warmers (Noah later told me they were called *Beats*), a skin fade haircut that looked out of place on his middle-aged head, along with a neat looking blue bomber jacket, skinny jeans and large, white Adidas trainers that seemed to announce his feet loudly to all around, despite them being the same colour as the snow all around us. And maybe the most peculiar, his skin had the clear orange glow of fake tan, despite the natural shade of his Spanish nationality. It was fairly evident that his young wife had a significant influence on his dress sense.

'My friend, my friend!' He repeated as he approached us. 'I want to talk to you. I heard you talked to my ex-wife today. I know you are investigating the murder, I don't want you to get a bad impression of me.'

We'd barely left the B&B; had they been on the phone to him as soon as we left? That was quick work. 'Hi Pedro, don't worry, I like to make my own impressions,' I reassured him as he reached us. 'How did you know that, have you spoken to Kimmy and Claire?'

'No, no, I haven't been friends with them for over a year!' He declared as he held his chest, catching his breath, obviously going along with the official version that they're no longer friends. 'I saw you together with her earlier, when I was clearing snow. I can guess what she has been saying.'

'Don't worry, Pedro, I took it with a pinch of salt,' I told him again. 'I do want to speak to you, though. I'm helping the police until they get here, so I'm speaking to everyone who was in the square this morning.' I'd decided to be upfront with why I was talking to everyone, seeing as they all seemed to be guessing anyway.

'Such sad business, poor Mrs Flowers,' he said, taking his headphones off as if it was a hat and he was showing a moment of respect. 'Of course I want to help. How about I walk with you both and we can go for a little drink? I'll tell you everything you need.'

I didn't want to spend yet more precious time consuming food and drink, and I'd hoped to find Reverend Flowers next, but I did need to speak to Pedro so I decided to seize the opportunity. 'Thank you, Pedro, that will be great.' I gestured to Alfie. 'You know my brother, Alfie, don't you?'

He laughed and grabbed Alfie's gloved hand, shaking it warmly. 'Of course I know Alfie, your family's pub is my favourite place in Chalk Gap! After *Pedro's* of course.' He winked and started to trudge towards the square.

He'd reached the end of the road and had to join the pavement where the square starts, which of course was still knee high in snow. 'I don't have a shovel I'm sorry, so you two will have to dig for us all if you don't mind.' To say he wasn't dressed for this weather was an understatement; I wondered how his skin tight jeans and ridiculous trainers would survive the depth of snow ahead of us.

'What would you like to know?' he asked me.

I decided not to tell him that I already knew anything from Claire and Kimmy (who he was pretending not to be friends with, in any case), to see if his account matched theirs. 'Just your story, from the beginning. Your relationship with Cherry, where Reverend Flowers fits in.'

'I loved Cherry very much,' he started as Alfie

and I trudged either side of him, starting to clear away the snowfall in front of us. 'I am very sorry for what I did to Gloria, but sometimes you fall in love and you can't help it.'

'What if that's what happened with Cherry and Reverend Flowers?' Alfie asked. I could tell he was playing devil's advocate to make a point; he was cheated on by his ex before Dylan and hated any kind of infidelity.

'What do you say?' He stopped and turned to Alfie, clenching his fists. 'That's not the same, my friend. That's not the same at all, don't say that please.'

'Okay, sorry,' my brother replied, as I shot him a look which told him to be quiet.

'Anyway, Cherry and I were perfect for each other. Perfect. She was so beautiful, and funny, and a kind person. We didn't mean to hurt anyone but we fell in love.' He smiled and I could tell he was reliving the memories, looking proud and sad at the same time. 'Have you two ever seen her? She's beautiful. I know every man in Chalk Gap is jealous, I bet you both are too. I bet she beats every woman either of you have ever known.'

Alfie and I exchanged a smirk over his shoulder. He was asking the wrong two people: an openly gay man and probably Chalk Gap's least experienced and least eligible bachelor, neither of us had much history with women to compare. He tried to take his phone from his pocket to presumably show us a picture, but seemed to forget that we were fighting our way through severe snow fall; he gave up when his screen got covered in white slush for the fourth time.

'Before the Reverend ruined all that, and took her away from me. It was his fault that I had to throw her out last night. We were happy and now she's gone.' It was interesting that he couldn't see the parallels with his own infidelity just a year or so before, but even more interesting that he seemed to blame Reverend Flowers and not Cherry herself. It was as if she was a possession that had been taken away from him. I wondered if he decided to take Frances away in return, before I remembered his alibi from Claire. It would be interesting to see how he dealt with that part of his story, seeing as he wasn't admitting to being friends with her and Kimmy.

'I don't want people to think badly of me,' he said, as if reading my mind. 'I know that Cherry and I caused very much hurt to Gloria. I'm sure many people think I am getting my just desserts back. But me and Gloria had been very unhappy for many years. I was wrong, I should have ended it sooner, but you met her this morning, Edward.' He paused long enough for his words to hang in the snowy air. 'She was a very difficult woman. It was not easy being married to her. But I did wrong and I'm sorry.'

I glanced at him next to me and considered him carefully, with his ridiculous haircut and glowing fake tan: he was the very definition of a male mid-life crisis. He seemed a pleasant enough man, and was thought of as kind and friendly by reputation in the village, but he had clearly lost his head and thought with the wrong body part.

'How did you find out about the affair?' I asked him next. His account of this was pretty much identical to the version from Kimmy and Claire, other than the way he framed the story continued to blame Reverend Flowers and not Cherry herself. But there was something I needed more information. 'What happened last night when you kicked her out?'

'I hope the Reverend isn't around. I don't want to see him,' Pedro answered, instead of starting his story. We were almost at the pub as we climbed through the snow in the square. He glanced over at the church as he resumed speaking. 'After I found out everything I did, I thought for a few days. But I couldn't live with it any longer. Even though I loved Cherry, I couldn't stay with a woman who was in another man's bed.'

'So you confronted her?' my brother asked.

'Yes, but not in an angry way. Not shouting and screaming. We sat down, I told her calmly what I knew and how disappointed I was. Then I told her it was over and I asked her to leave.'

'Is that it?' Alfie questioned, clearly getting into the drama of the situation. 'Did she admit it, did she deny it? She didn't just agree to leave?'

Pedro answered without looking at either of us. 'Yes, she denied it, she kept denying it, but I knew it was true. We argued a little but I was trying not to get angry. Then she said she didn't want to stay with someone who didn't trust her. So she packed her things and left.'

I wanted to move on to what happened this morning, and asked about the incident on the square and what led up to it. Again, his story matched the one given by Claire; he'd got drunk after she left, woke up this morning and decided to confront Reverend Flowers. Once more it was interesting to see which of the two parties he'd took his anger out on.

'So what happened after the incident with Reverend Flowers? Where did you go?'

We'd reached the pub now and we stood at the doorway as he made eye contact with me. 'Edward, I suppose I should be honest.'

'Please do.'

'The snow was getting very deep already then and it was already difficult to get far. I got to the high street but I sat on a wall and thought about everything. I got very upset. Anyway, the part I wasn't honest about is that I am still friends with Kimmy and Claire Atkinson. But please keep that to yourself as I don't want to make trouble for them with Gloria.'

I nodded that I understood as he continued. 'I need to tell you that to explain where I was. The wall I was sat on was just further down the street than the B&B. I went and knocked on the door, but when they didn't answer I sat and waited on their doorstep. Soon Claire came back and let me in, and then I was with her for the next hour.'

Another part of the story that matched exactly, and if both parties were telling the truth, he couldn't have killed Frances. 'Anyway, I want to buy you a drink now,' Pedro added, pointing towards the pub door.

'I hate you, I hate you! You ruined everything!' We looked to see Jacob Flowers across the square, at the foot of the West Chalk Cliff. I waited a second to see what would happen, anticipating him coming to attack again, but this time he stayed still. 'I hope you're happy now!' He roared across the snow, with anger and upset in his voice.

'The boy has just lost his mother,' Pedro said quietly to us. 'I'm not going to argue with him. Let's go inside. Come on.'

'Why don't you go in with Alfie,' I suggested. 'I'll make sure he's alright.' They nodded in agreement and went into the pub.

'Coward!' Jacob yelled across to the doorway where only I now stood. 'Everything is ruined.

Everything!'

You might know that I'm not always comfort-able in these situations when emotions are high, but I'd like to think I was getting better. I called out to him. 'It's okay, Jacob, he's gone. But you and I can have a chat if you like.' I started to move slowly towards him through the thick white sheets in front of me.

'Stay away, stay away! I don't want to talk. It's too late.' And with that, he turned and started scrambling up the cliff path behind him. He was young and nimble, so seemed to move quite quickly, but the snow was deep and dangerous looking. He wasn't safe and I didn't know his in-tentions, and before I knew it I found myself going after him.

'Stop, wait!' I shouted as I scrambled through the snow partway up the cliff path. I was evi-dently a much less able climber than Jacob and had already fallen onto all fours, trying and failing to pick myself up.

'Go away, leave me alone!' He screamed from above me.

'It's not safe up here,' I called back. 'I just need to know you're safe.'

'For god's sake, I'm fine!' He shouted as he turned to face me. 'I'm not going to do anything, I just want you to leave me alone. You're all so stu-pid.'

And with that, he turned in the direction of the Church and started to climb down in a completely different direction away from me and towards it. I watched him reach the bottom and saunter back across the Churchyard path into the Vicarage. He was safe.

But I wasn't. I suddenly realised in a panic that I was partway up the snow-drenched cliff path in quite a precarious position. I took a breath, ignored the sudden panic I could feel inside, and tried to slowly climb back down to the ground. I started to shiver but didn't know if this was through cold or nerves. I just tried to focus on remaining steady and moving one foot at a time to safety.

I felt a little more confident as I got a little closer to the square, so I started to speed up a little. But that proved to be a mistake. I lost my balance and tumbled to my left, off the main path, in a blur of snow, anxiety and panic.

I landed in a heap in a far corner of the square, behind the pub and out of view from the main square. And that's when I saw the second body.

17

'I don't like this Edward, mate. I don't like this one bit. Two murders now and we still can't get through.'

If even DI Appleby was starting to panic, I couldn't begin to process how I felt. Our snow day in Chalk Gap, which everyone had expected to be a magical winter wonderland, had turned into a twisted, ice-tinted horror show: with us all trapped in the village with the killer, who had now claimed two victims.

After spending the last few hours looking into Frances Flowers' murder and making headway with more than half of the main suspects / witnesses (even if the headway being that all four people I'd spoken to had alibis for the timeframe of Frances' death), I felt like we were back to square one. As I stood looking on while on video call to Appleby, PC Wood and Doctor Albright were once again liaising remotely with Appleby's colleagues to confirm the death.

The victim was, perhaps unsurprisingly in hindsight, Cherry McDonald. When I'd fallen to the bottom of the cliff path, I saw something ominous sticking out of the snow near where I'd landed. It was her hand. I'd later wondered if she wasn't quite dead when left under the snow and had managed to push her hand through, or if the killer had done it so she'd be eventually discovered by anyone that managed to stumble onto (quite literally in my case) that secluded corner under the cliff.

I'd moved just enough snow out of the way to identify who the person was by her face (though I didn't know Cherry to speak to, I knew her by sight) but otherwise left everything exactly as it was so as not to disturb the body. What we didn't know yet was when she was murdered or how long she'd been there; I was hoping the current remote work on the crime scene might shed some light, but again this was difficult without the proper professionals being able to access it.

However, one thing I did notice when I was trying to identify who it was: glowing red, tell-tale marks on her neck. It appeared that she'd been strangled.

This new murder certainly raised lots of new questions, despite all the questions about the original murder remaining unanswered. I say 'new murder': there was every possibility that Cherry was killed first, we just didn't know. And this was something Appleby was becoming increasingly frustrated with.

'What is going on, mate? One woman battered to death with a shovel. Another strangled to death and hidden in the snow. Their husbands in a big public confrontation this morning, one accusing the other of sleeping with his wife. Now both wives are dead. Not to mention one of these men is the local Vicar. Are the two murders connected? Which happened first? Were they even committed by the same person?' He stopped and let out a deep sigh. I looked at the screen to see him rub his hand over his face in anger. 'We don't know the answer to any of these questions, because we can't access the bloody crime scenes. We've got a junior constable, a local GP and a school librarian turned amateur detective trying to do the work for us. No offence, mate.'

His words stung as I sat in that cold, empty church hall. My old nemesis, anxiety, was already creeping up to say hello when I had one murder to solve without the police. Now that it was two, he'd not just said hello, he'd let himself into my house and was living there rent-free.

But then I remembered Dad's words from earlier. I could do this. 'Look, Appleby. You asked me to help because you couldn't get through. You still can't, so I'm the best you've got. Yes, I was expecting only one murder to investigate, and no, I don't know what's going on here but I'm going to find out. I've done it before and I'll do it again.'

And then I breathed. I didn't know where that

came from, or even if I believed it myself. But Appleby seemed to.

'You're right, mate, I'm sorry. It's just so annoying not being able to get involved. Update me on how it's going with the Vicar's wife, then we'll work out a plan for this new development.'

New development – it sounded so clinical and impersonal, not that a young woman with her whole life ahead of her was lying dead in the snow. But I ignored his poor wording and gave him the highlights of my investigations so far: that Gloria was convinced it was Pedro, but he had an alibi (as did Gloria herself, along with Kimmy and Claire); Pedro and Cherry were actually married; the alleged affair between Cherry and Reverend Flowers seemed to be true; Flowers seemed to have a hold over his friendship group, so much so that Kimmy and Claire had to lie about being friends with Pedro; and Pedro told us he kicked Cherry out the night before, and as far as he knew she left the village.

Appleby listened to all of this carefully, but barely let me finish speaking before giving his view. 'The affair definitely links these two murders, mate. They're not separate incidents. I'd swear they're done by the same person, even though the methods are different.'

'They're not that different though, are they?' I'd been thinking about this for the last twenty

minutes or since I'd found Cherry. 'Hitting someone with a shovel that happened to be around,
using only their bare hands to strangle someone.
Both methods suggest a quick, unplanned, spare of
the moment murder. Or are meant to create the
impression of it.'

'That's a good point, actually,' he conceded.
'You think the Vicar then? I'd say either him or
this Pedro, but he has an alibi for the Vicar's wife.
And if it *was* someone else who killed her - right
at their back door, where they were arguing moments before - where did the Vicar go? It's gotta be
him.'

I'd of course considered this myself, but I wasn't
sure yet. It seemed a little obvious. 'Why would
Reverend Flowers kill both women, though? Even
if he didn't love Frances anymore, that probably
means he loved Cherry.' Of course I could think of
several scenarios where the affair had turned sour,
but I was playing devil's advocate.

'Mate, you don't see this stuff all the time like
I do,' he said, as I tried not to get angry at his
patronising tone. 'You think the local Vicar wants
a scandal like that? What if this Cherry girl was
threatening to tell his wife, and he never planned
on this being more than a bit on the side? Remember we don't know how long Cherry's been there,
she could have come to him last night after Pedro
kicked her out, and then he's killed her to keep the
affair quiet. Yeah, I bet that's exactly what's hap-

pened.'

Perhaps he was right. A Miss Marple quote came to mind, one that Noah often used: 'I know that in crime novels it is always the most unlikely person. But I never find that rule applies in real life.' Maybe it was true in this case, but I didn't want to condemn the Vicar without knowing everything. I hadn't even spoken to him yet, which was the next point I made to Appleby.

'Yeah, that's a fair point, mate. You need to make that a priority I'd say,' he said, sounding a little less stressed and a little more confident. 'And obviously keep an eye on the others, too. I mean it's very convenient Pedro has an alibi. Do you think this lesbian couple are telling the truth?'

'I don't see any reason why not,' I said. But it was something that had occurred to me too; they'd admitted their friendship with Pedro, it wasn't beyond the realms of possibility that Claire had given him a false alibi, even if she didn't think he was the killer.

'Like I said, mate, I don't like this – these suspects wandering round freely while we can't get through.' I didn't point out that they couldn't wander very far. 'This situation is so unprecedented, though – let me check out what we're able to do, if I'm able to keep them all in one place with PC Wood watching them, once he's finished up on the crime scene. We don't want another murder.'

'Who are we officially including in that list, then?' I asked. 'Obviously Flowers and Pedro, along with Gloria, Claire and Kimmy. But Jacob Flowers is still looming round angrily, and I still haven't had chance to speak to Everest Brown yet either.'

'Speak to him when you can, but I don't think he's important, mate. The son's worth speaking to, though – might be able to tell you a bit more about his Dad's behaviour. I'll also get PC Wood to escort you back to the crime scene in the Vicarage back-yard, see what you can find there. But let's wait til they've confirmed the second death so you can look at both scenes at once.'

As I looked on at the crime scene, I saw PC Wood start to put tape around the area in question. Within seconds, I saw movement in the pub back window which overlooked the bottom of the cliff: Mum trying to get the latest gossip, no doubt. I rounded up the conversation with Appleby quickly, promising to update him later. There was someone I had to speak to quickly, before he found out from someone else. I had to go and tell Pedro Hernandez that his wife had been murdered.

18

'Edward, Edward, what's going on out there? Do we have a serial killer running round? And we're trapped in the village with him? We're all fearing for our safety in here. '

'There's been a second body, hasn't there? Do we have two murders to investigate now?'

Claire, Kimmy and I had barely stepped into the pub when I had Mum and Noah bombarding me trying to find out what was going on. But I had to tell Pedro first, before I spoke to anyone else. It was the right thing to do.

The exception I'd made was to confide in Kimmy and Claire; I didn't imagine breaking news of this kind would be something I'd be good at, particularly as I didn't know Pedro very well, so I'd told them first and they'd come along to help break the news to him. But I had to get past Mum and Noah first.

'I'm sorry, guys, I just need to speak to someone.' I spied Pedro sat by the fireplace with Patrick, who I guessed had swapped with Alfie so he could go back to guarding the crime scene with Dylan; Pedro must have wondered where I'd got to, but luckily their seats weren't in view of the back windows.

Mum followed my gaze across the pub and I saw the penny drop. 'Wait a minute, that must mean that it's...'

I nodded quietly. 'Please, Mum, he has to know first. Just let me speak to him.'

'Of course, love, of course. I can be tactful, you know.' She stopped to look indignant before putting her sympathetic face back on. 'I just can't believe it. Poor Patrick. He's not even been seeing her that long.'

'Mum, no! It's not Becky -'

'That would make no sense, Linda,' Noah interrupted. 'Think about it. The whole mystery revolves around the affair accusation. If there's a second body, it's going to be linked to that. Look who Patrick is sat with.'

'Oh my god, you're right! So it's -'

Both of you, please,' I said, waving my arms and shushing them desperately.

'Edward, shall we...' Claire gestured tactfully over to Pedro, suggesting we should get a move on. But it was too late. He was coming over.

'Please,' I whispered again. 'Let me do this right. And we need to use the flat too.'

'Yes, love, yes, of course. The poor man,' Mum

replied in hushed tones.

'Edward, my friend, where have you been all this time?' He stopped and saw all of our faces. 'Wait, what is wrong? What is going on?'

Claire stepped forward and took charge. 'Pedro, we need to speak to you. But shall we go upstairs to Linda's flat?'

'Oh, for god's sake, just tell him.' We all turned to see Gloria behind us in the doorway, before she stepped forward menacingly. 'It won't be a surprise anyway, he probably killed her.'

He looked puzzled. 'Who, Frances? I didn't, I have an alibi, Edward knows this and will tell the police.'

'Still acting dumb, are we?' she said mockingly with an evil-looking grin on her face. 'No, not Frances, you idiot -'

'Gloria, enough!' Claire bellowed, the usually quietly spoken lady surprising all of us.

'Yes, just shut up,' Kimmy added.

'What is she talking about?' Pedro asked, looking around at everyone. Claire and Kimmy bowed their heads, Mum looked away, Noah attempted a sympathetic half-smile. Just Gloria met his eyes, looking straight at him defiantly. I saw the confusion on his face change to outright horror as he realised.

'No, no, no, no, no, no, no, no, no, no, no, no,

no, no, no,' he uttered to himself in a deadly low, quiet, manic tone as he put his hands over his mouth and rocked on the spot. 'Not my Cherry, not my Cherry, not my Cherry.'

'Yes, your Cherry,' Gloria raged at him. 'As you well know, seeing as you killed her in jealous rage. And poor Frances Flowers too.'

He looked at her in distraught disbelief. 'No, no, don't say that, I couldn't... not my Cherry, I couldn't, I couldn't.'

'Oh, but you could kill Frances Flowers, is that what you're saying?' she retorted with a sneer.

'No, I didn't kill anyone, I already said, I was with Claire at the B&B, Edward knows this.' He looked at me desperately.

'Oh don't worry, I already know those two are friends with you behind my back!' She shot a deathly look at Claire and Kimmy as she said that. 'Got Claire to lie for you, have you?'

'No he has not!' Claire said, stepping towards her. 'Now, stop this, Gloria, right now. You can't behave like this. He's just found out his wife is dead. Two of our friends are dead.'

'One of our friends and one little tramp!' Gloria shouted spitefully.

'How dare you, how dare you!' Pedro leapt forward but luckily Patrick grabbed him.

'What are you going to do, kill me as well?' she

sniped back.

'Right you, that's enough!' Mum said, finally stepping forward. I was surprised she'd let this go on as long as it had, but I suspect she was enjoying the drama. 'He's just found Cherry's died. She's lying out there in the cold, for god's sake, have some respect!'

Gloria moved towards Mum, meeting her glare. 'Oh that's rich coming from you. Don't pretend you're not enjoying the gossip, you nosy old cow.'

Mum looked at her for a split second, in obvious disbelief, before taking a step back. And then she slapped her right across the face. 'Now get out and leave us all alone.'

Gloria looked livid as she rubbed her hand across her cheek. 'You'll pay for this, Linda Crisp. As soon as the police get here, I'm going to have them arrest you.' She next turned her attention to her ex-husband. 'And you, you've got what you deserve. Even if you do have an alibi and didn't physically kill either of them, you as good as did with your stupid jealous tantrum. Reverend Flowers is a good man. I swear, if you've caused that man to do anything -'

I didn't get chance at the time to reflect on how odd that remark was, as she was interrupted.

'Excuse me, did you mention the police? Because that's me.' PC Wood was stood behind her with a shy smile on his face. 'Edward, I've got word from DI Appleby that we should keep the suspects under supervision in the church hall, until he can get through to formally question them. So I'm sorry, everyone, you're going to have to come with me.'

19

'Suspects? This is outrageous, you can't keep us here. It's not like we can go anywhere anyway, have you seen how deep that snow is outside? Bloody idiots!'

Gloria had reacted as well as you might predict about being classed as a suspect and kept in the freezing cold church hall. PC Wood had made the announcement much less diplomatically than I might have, so I'd tried to diffuse the situation by explaining that our 'suspects' were merely derived from the list of people who were present in the square during the incident this morning with Pedro and Reverend Flowers.

Pedro had come along without fuss, saying that he'd do anything to clear his name and get justice for Cherry. Similarly, Claire and Kimmy were happy to help with the enquiries and also got to stay with Pedro to make sure he was okay. We'd picked up Everest Brown from his burger van outside, though I still needed to speak to him to see if he had any bearing on the case. Neither Reverend or Jacob Flowers were present yet, but we had one more person present this morning who had insisted she was a suspect.

'Honestly, Edward, you can't be excluding me just because I'm your mother. I was there this morning, so it's only fair I'm treated as a suspect like everyone else.' Nothing to do with being able to get the latest gossip first hand, I thought.

Otherwise, we were just missing Reverend and Jacob Flowers. I'd left PC Wood supervising the group (with Noah's help) and I was on my way to the Vicarage - just down the path from the church hall, but still a difficult trek in the thick snow - to see if I could find either of them. As I passed the church, I noticed the door open and the light on in the foyer.

As I stepped into the building, I could hear a murmuring voice and soon saw the back of the Vicar's head. He was knelt down in one of the pews, leaning forward with his head resting on his closed hands. I couldn't hear what he was saying but it was clear they were prayers.

I needed to speak to him, urgently, but I couldn't interrupt a grieving man in prayer. I decided to try the Vicarage to see if Jacob was home, then try the Reverend again on the way back. I turned back towards the door when I heard a voice travel across the building, echoing with the church acoustics.

'Please, don't go on my account. If the church is open, it is open for everyone.' He stood up and turned to see who it was. 'Edward, come and join me. I thought you'd come and find me sooner or later. I know we need to speak.'

His voice sounded outwardly jovial but I knew that couldn't be his true emotion right now. I approached cautiously, not knowing what to expect from the second grieving husband I'd encountered that day. There was a good chance that one of them wasn't actually grieving and they were really the killer. Could it be the Reverend? He certainly seemed to be number one suspect and was Appleby's pick. But I wanted to keep an open mind.

'Sorry to disturb you, Reverend. And I haven't had chance to say again since earlier, I'm sorry about your wife.'

'Thank you Edward, it's okay. God sometimes moves in mysterious ways, I'm afraid.' He returned to his seat in the pew and beckoned for me to do the same. 'I just heard about Cherry McDonald too, another tragedy. I came here to offer a prayer for her.'

We remained in silence for a few moments. I played his words about Cherry over in my head but I couldn't detect anything from his pleasant, sympathetic tone. Were these the words of a kindly Reverend sad to see a young life end, while grieving for his beloved wife? Or was his true grief for Cherry, as his lover? He wasn't giving anything away with the way he spoke about her, which I'm sure was intentional.

'We haven't spent much time together over the years, you and I, have we?' he said. I wasn't sure if he was going somewhere with this or just meaninglessly filling the silence. 'I've seen you grow up, though. From a teenager, to a young man, to the man you are today. And your work with the police has been outstanding, I must say. The way you solved the murder of the Head Teacher like that. It made me very proud to know you.'

'Thank you, Reverend.' I didn't know what else to do with this flattery other than thank him. I was still dissecting his words about Cherry before this, and wondering how he knew about her death so quickly. I decided to move the conversation on. 'I'm sorry, but I need to ask you -'

'You don't need to ask me anything, Edward. I'll tell you everything you need to know, quite gladly. I know you're a good man and you won't want to ask awkward questions on the day I've lost my wife. This way you won't need to.' I could see what Claire and Kimmy meant about his tendency for control. 'Firstly, I was not having an affair with Cherry McDonald. Pedro Gonzalez got it wrong. Plain and simple.'

'Who do you think she was having the affair with?' I asked in reply.

He looked surprised by this, he'd clearly expected me to accept his answer and move on. 'I have no idea, but it wasn't me.'

'Of course, Reverend. Just that Pedro was certain he'd caught Cherry coming to the Vicarage when Mrs Flowers was at work, and a couple of other witnesses shared their suspicions too.' I wanted to show him I was a worthy opponent and that he couldn't strong-arm me, but I feared I'd pushed it too far.

He stood up in the pew and peered down his glasses at me. 'Edward, I think I'm right in saying you have no official authority on this case. And I'm sure that after several hours now, and with two bodies and a killer on the loose, the police will manage to get through. Therefore, I think it best to wait for the police. I have nothing more to say to you.'

'Actually, the police have asked that all suspects wait under supervision in the church hall, I was going to escort you there after we'd spoken -'

'If that's the case, I'll check with my friend the DCI and be along once I've spoken to him. Now I'd like you to leave please.' His voice was firm and authoritative; I'd really touched a nerve.

'Okay, I'm going. And I'm sorry if I upset you. I'm just trying to find out what happened,' I managed as he started to usher me out. 'Just one more thing, do you know where Jacob is? We need him to come to the church hall with you, once you've spoken to the DCI.'

'Don't you dare bring my son into this, he has nothing to do with it,' he boomed. 'Now get out!'

After I left, I stood outside the church door a few moments trying to process what just happened. To say that hadn't gone to plan was an understatement. I wasn't expecting that reaction at all. Even Gloria had played along with my questions eventually after having her fun.

But I knew what I had to work out in my head: was this a man with something to hide, or a grieving man who had just reached the end of his tether? I don't know why but I found myself stepping back into the church foyer. I'm not sure looking back what I had in mind when I did that: to try and speak to Reverend Flowers again, or to see if he resumed praying or what. I just had a strong feeling that I'd left the conversation unresolved and I needed to go back.

I could hear his voice again as I walked through the foyer. But it was louder this time and I soon realised he wasn't praying. He was on the phone.

'We have a problem. Edward Crisp has just been to see me poking round. I think he knows about the affair.'

20

Who was he talking to? It couldn't be Cherry, who he'd been accused of having the affair with, unless his abilities as a Vicar included being able to communicate with those beyond the grave.

I thought of those he was likely to confide in and had an idea. Luckily, most of the options were being supervised next door in the church hall.

Immediately on my return, I went straight to PC Wood. 'Has anyone in this room used their phone in the last few minutes?'

'No, mate, not at all. I've had my eye on them the whole time,' he said a little too brightly and enthusiastically. He was a terrible liar.

'Dean,' I said sternly. 'This is important to the investigation. You don't want DI Appleby to find out you were assisting a suspect.'

'It wasn't like that… I mean, I'd never do that.'

'Dean,' I repeated, trying to sound as stern as I could.

'I promised I wouldn't say,' he replied weakly.

'Who was it?'

He sighed and looked down at the floor, embarrassed and defeated. 'It was the bossy lady with all the perfume.'

Gloria Hernandez. Of course it was.

A couple of minutes later, Noah and I were in the small room off the main church hall with Gloria. I'd decided to bring Noah with me as he hadn't been directly involved for a while, and I wasn't sure I could face the full force of Gloria on my own. Besides, I was tired of Gloria being difficult and I knew it would annoy her.

'If you must know, I had to ring my elderly mother to check she was okay. She lives the other side of the village and I was worried about her. You *have* seen the snow outside, haven't you, Edward?'

I couldn't believe Gloria could answer me with such disdain in her voice when she was blatantly lying, but I was ready for her. 'That's fine, Gloria, that makes sense. And I hope your mum is okay. But are you alright just to show me your phone, so I can see the call?'

Our eyes met in a deadly battle of wills. She knew what game I was playing and she was planning her next move. But when she took it, it wasn't one I was expecting. She burst into tears.

'Are you okay?' Noah asked. 'Why are you upset? Are you going to confess to the murder?'

She looked up and gave him the most deathly stare, as if she was about to commit another one. I nudged him to be quiet but he didn't take the hint.

'What? We're due to have a plot twist in the case, and I just thought that would be a good one.' He smiled brightly at me.

'Sorry, what?' she muttered as she wiped her eyes. 'What is he going on about? It's bad enough you've seen me like this, without him talking absolute rubbish.'

'That's okay, Gloria. Don't worry about him,' I tried to say as firmly as I could (I'd been doing well but her crying outburst had thrown me). 'Whatever you're upset about, I can help. Just tell me whatever it is you know.'

'Ah yes, you'd love that, wouldn't you? If you were such a good detective, you wouldn't need my help.'

'Your help?' She was exasperating. 'Gloria, you're meant to be under supervision here for a reason. Yet you managed to con PC Wood into going to make a phone call. A phone call I heard the other end of. It was to Reverend Flowers. Saying he thinks I know about 'the affair.' The affair that you earlier said definitely wasn't true, and since then the other party in the affair has been found dead. Now, it's up to you if you wait for CID or tell me, but either way you've been caught out and you're going to have to explain what's going on.'

She examined me for a second and burst out laughing. 'Edward Crisp, you have been working on your assertiveness, haven't you? Fine. Young man, do you want to get your little phone app ready to note what I say?'

Noah nodded enthusiastically and opened up notes on his phone, completely missing her sarcasm.

She played with her bright fluorescent fingernails, clearly thinking of how to start. 'I first want to say that Reverend Flowers is a good man, one of the best I've met. And what I'm about to say doesn't make him a killer. I still think it's my awful ex-husband, he clearly got Claire to lie about his alibi for Frances' murder.'

I wanted her to stick to the story in hand. 'But about Reverend Flowers, what were you going to say?'

She picked at her nails again. 'No. I won't do it. I won't break a confidence like that. I'm not going to talk.'

'Gloria, you escaped police supervision to answer his call, and I already know his end of the conversation. So it's not even breaking confidence, not really. Just confirming for us.'

She stamped her feet on the floor from her chair. 'Fine. Yes it was me who he spoke to. And yes, he told me that he thought you knew about the affair.'

'His affair with Cherry McDonald?' I knew this but I wanted her to explicitly say which affair she was referring to:

'Yes, for God's sake, yes, do you want me to draw a picture? Yes, he was having an affair with Cherry McDonald. I was the only one who knew about it. And…'

'And what?'

'Nothing, never mind.'

This woman was exhausting. 'Gloria, what?'

She stayed quiet for what seemed like an eternity. 'Damn you, Edward Crisp, I'll say this to you off the record but I won't say it to the police, do you hear? I'll deny everything.'

'Deny what?'

'I want it to be my ex-husband, I really do. But I suppose,' she let out a deep sigh. 'I suppose it's very unlikely that Claire is lying about him being with her the time of the murder.' Even though she'd just accused Claire of this exact thing about a minute ago.

'I'm just worried. I mean, the Reverend has been acting out of character for weeks, this whole affair is out of character. What if he did it, Edward? What if Reverend Flowers killed them both?'

21

'I wonder if it is Reverend Flowers then? There are plenty of classic Agatha Christie mysteries where it is the obvious person, just with a few twists along the way.'

Noah, as usual forgetting we were in earshot of everyone, was enjoying the latest 'plot twist' that Gloria had confirmed the Reverend Flowers / Cherry affair and now suspected him. PC Wood had been called back to the crime scene so the two of us were supervising the suspects for a few minutes. As soon as he came back, I wanted to speak to everyone else in the room again in light of Cherry's murder.

DI Appleby had confirmed that the police were getting closer to getting through to the village; the farmers' tractors with fitted snow ploughs had arrived at the other end and were partway up the two miles of Chalk Gap Road from the A259, but it was a long process in the still falling deep snow.

Gloria was sitting in front of us looking worried. She was probably terrified of when Reverend Flowers arrived and would find out what she'd said.

Apparently, he'd confided in her only a few days ago, when he finally got round to having a moral crisis about it. He said he loved his wife dearly, knew he'd made a mistake, wanted to put an end to it and avoid a scandal without hurting Cherry's feelings. I'd wondered about Gloria's views on marital affairs, considering what happened to her and that it involved one of the same parties, but she just seemed to think Pedro was getting the karma he deserved. Even though she was now beginning to suspect the Reverend of the murders.

'I always forget to whisper when the suspects are near, I'm sorry,' Noah continued, still not even remotely whispering. 'I still think we have more plot twists to come in this mystery. Hopefully the crime scene will give us some new information too. It's very exciting though, isn't it? Us all trapped in the snowstorm and a killer on the loose. The murders might not be over yet.'

'Don't say that, darling,' Mum called out from across the room, not even pretending to not be listening. 'That's what I'm worried about. It seems a bit odd, doesn't it, that we're all stranded in the snow and suddenly the killings start. All women too. What if this affair thing is just a big coincidence and it's one of those serial killers? I'm staying in a big group from now on.'

Claire shot Mum a look as her and Kimmy comforted Pedro, who looked distraught. 'My Cherry, murdered by a serial killer? No, no, no, please don't say that... it's not possible!'

'I'm sorry, love, of course she hasn't, I'm so sorry.' Mum, for once, looked embarrassed and apologetic; I think she forgot Pedro was there. 'It's just terrifying to think that there's murder in our lovely little village again, but this time double murder, and it's nice people too! I just can't get used to the idea that it's someone we know doing this, I do hope it's a stranger.'

'It won't be a stranger, it will be someone you know,' Everest Brown spoke out for the first time. I looked over at him and he was leaning back on his chair, arms behind his head and one leg crossed over the other.

'You don't know that,' Mum replied. 'Look at you sitting over there, too cool for school in your beanie hat and your fancy knitwear. You're only saying that 'cos you're a stranger to the village yourself! Maybe it's you.'

'Mum, that's enough,' I said, with as much authority as I could manage.

'That's alright,' he said. 'The rest of you all know each other very well, it's natural that people will suspect me. I've been expecting it. But actually, I'm not a stranger. I have family here in the village.'

'No you haven't!' Mum retorted straight away. 'You're staying in the B&B. And anyway if you had family, we'd know them. Who are they then?'

'I, erm, I can't say,' he said weakly, sitting up and uncrossing his legs. He turned his head away to signify his involvement in the conversation was over. I also noticed a look between Kimmy and Claire and wondered how much they knew about their guest.

'That's who you should be looking at next, Edward, if you ask me,' Mum whispered to me, only doing a slightly better job of it than Noah, though I'm not sure why she'd bothered to whisper when she'd just said as much to Everest's face.

I was glad to have the distraction of PC Wood returning. I could see he was carrying something in a transparent plastic bag and looked flustered, so I walked towards the door and away from everyone so we could speak more confidentially. But I needn't have bothered as he called out to me from the doorway as he waved the bag around. 'Got a little something for you from the crime scene, mate!' Was I the only one present with any common sense today?

'Oh yes, how exciting!' Noah exclaimed. 'What is it?'

'Cherry McDonald's mobile phone,' he replied just as loudly before I could stop him. In front of all the suspects too; I couldn't believe a PC could be so incompetent.

'Ssshh, both of you!' I hissed. 'PC Wood, stay there, let's talk in the foyer please.'

'Oh okay, mate, no worries,' he replied in his usual jolly way, not even realising the problem.

Noah came to follow but I nodded my head for him to stay in the main hall with the others. He looked disappointed but nodded back.

'A couple of messages from Appleby, mate,' Wood said as soon as we set foot in the foyer; he was no quieter but at least we were in a different room. 'First, he said to tell you they're further along Chalk Gap Road now and are hoping to be here in an hour or so, though it's still not guaranteed. Next, he told me to give you Cherry's mobile phone. The Doctor and I found it in her pocket. He wants you to look at it. But he's not sure if he's supposed to, and he doesn't want to get fired, so keep it quiet.'

This situation was getting worse. Now I was looking at evidence from the crime scene that I wasn't supposed to handle, and the police might or might not get through in the next hour, while we had two bodies now and a killer on the loose who might or might not be in the same building as me that moment.

'Are you okay, mate?' Wood asked. 'You look a little stressed. I know what you're going through, we're doing a lot, aren't we? I've never been so involved in a crime scene before. It's scary but quite exciting at the same time. This is what I signed up for. I finally feel like a real copper and not just the village policeman dealing with stolen bikes.'

In that moment, PC Wood reminded me a little of Noah. He was still fairly young – he couldn't have been older than 23 or 24 – and had a definite naivety about him, but I could tell that he wanted to be a good policeman and that one day he would be.

'You're doing really well,' I reassured him. 'I'll make sure I tell DI Appleby when he gets here. You should be really proud of yourself.'

'Thanks mate, I appreciate that,' he said warmly as he shook my hand with his overly strong handshake again.

We returned to the hall to find Claire and Kimmy coming straight over to me. 'Can we speak to you please, Edward?' Claire asked.

I agreed and took them to the little room I'd spoken to Gloria in earlier. 'Is everything alright, have you remembered something else?' I asked as we sat down. I noticed straight away how nervous Kimmy looked.

'We wanted your advice really, Edward,' Claire started, with her hand over Kimmy's. 'If there's something involving one of us that might get found out by the police later, do you think it's better if we tell you now so we can explain it properly?'

I remembered my fear earlier about not wanting one of these two lovely ladies to be the killer. 'Yes of course, what is it?'

'Okay, Kimmy, that's my bit,' Claire said to her wife, still keeping hold of her hand. 'You're up.'

Kimmy took a deep breath and I felt her nerves strongly. 'I... I couldn't help but overhear that they found Cherry's phone. The thing is, there might be something on there that might incriminate me.'

22

'I don't know where to start,' Kimmy mumbled nervously.

'Just tell him what happened, it will be fine,' Claire coaxed her gently.

'I needed to borrow money,' Kimmy said. 'I'd got Claire lots of lovely things for Christmas, and some bits and pieces to spruce up the B&B. I know I shouldn't spend what I can't afford, I just wanted to have a nice Christmas and -'

'... and she got a bit carried away,' Claire finished for her.

'Oh don't, I feel awful,' Kimmy whined. 'I should have told you, I should have come to you.'

'But you didn't, it's okay. Just tell him,' Claire said. She still had her usual gentle tone in her voice but she sounded firm.

'Okay, sorry. Anyway, I got myself into some trouble with payday loans. It's so easy to get approved for them, and you just think you have plenty of time to pay them back. But when you can't and they start adding interest, oh, it was just all such a mess!' I could tell she was getting herself into a state. "I'm sorry, Claire, I messed everything up!'

'It's okay,' Claire repeated, clasping Kimmy's hand a little tighter now. It was embarrassing for all three of us for to have to them air their dirty laundry like this. 'Edward doesn't need to know all that, let's just focus on the Cherry part.'

'I didn't know what to do. I know I should have gone straight to Claire but I wanted to sort it without worrying her. I tried to think of who out of our friends might be able to help me out. I didn't want to ask the Flowers as I thought they might think it was a sin getting into debt like that.' I glanced at Claire and could see she was doing her best to remain supportive and not get annoyed. I liked Kimmy from the time I'd spent with her that day, but I could see she was a quite silly woman, almost like a big grown-up child.

'I know that Pedro doesn't have any money of his own, we're always comparing how bad our financial situations are. So I made the mistake of asking Gloria.'

'That didn't go well?' I asked. I can't imagine that it did.

'No, she just said no outright. I don't know if it's because she couldn't afford it or just didn't want to. But I made the mistake of telling her the story while I was asking, and that Claire didn't know. Every time we've been all together since, she makes little jibes about it in front of Claire, as if she's going to tell her.'

'We need to stop being friends with that woman,' Claire said.

'She can be nice sometimes,' Kimmy replied weakly.

'Kimmy, stop seeing the good in people like Gloria,' Claire said. 'I don't know why you bother. Even today she conned you into helping her sell her stupid sweets.'

'Anyway,' Kimmy said, seemingly about to finally get to the point. 'After that I remembered that Cherry had some money behind her. And she was always very nice to us, so I thought I'd give her a try. She was so kind and understanding, she said yes straightaway and listened to all my problems about it.'

'How does this link to her phone then?' I was keen for Kimmy to get to the point.

'I thought I'd be able to pay her back in instalments, and she said there was no rush, but I couldn't make the first month or the second. She was very nice about it and said we could sort it out, but in the last couple of weeks I've got myself into a bit more trouble and I've been talking to Cherry about it.'

'Baby, don't just tell him you were talking to her about it, you have to tell him the full story,'

Claire said. She still sounded pleasant enough but I noticed she'd moved her hand away.

'Okay, so I asked her to borrow more money. But she said no. She wasn't horrible about it but she said she thought it was best I tell Claire. But I got a bit defensive about it and it turned into a bit of an argument, I misunderstood and thought she was threatening to tell Claire herself. But when I read it back once I calmed down, she wasn't. She was just trying to help.'

'Read it back?' I asked.

'Yes, all of this in the last few days was by text message.' Ah, this made sense – she was worried about the incriminating messages on Cherry's phone.

'Tell him the last part,' Claire instructed.

'I was just in such a mess, I said things to her I shouldn't have, when I thought she was having a go at me. I told her she wasn't getting a penny of her money and if she said anything to Claire she'd be sorry. I don't know what came over me.' Finally, she broke down and sobbed.

'It's okay, don't get upset,' I said, as kindly as I could in my embarrassment. 'When were the last of these messages?'

Kimmy was still a sobbing mess so Claire answered for her. 'Yesterday.'

'And when did Kimmy tell you, Claire?'

'Only just now,' Claire replied. 'She thought she better tell me the whole story because she thought she'd be a suspect for Cherry's murder.' Kimmy let out a loud wail.

This was interesting. Clearly, Kimmy had only confessed this (both to me and Claire) as she knew that the phone would reveal it anyway; it made me wonder what else the phone would tell us, and what other secrets this group of people had. This thought reminded me to use the opportunity to find out what I could while I had them here, particularly about Cherry; I didn't know too much about her and apart from the grieving Pedro these two were my best hope.

'Was Cherry a kind person, then?' I asked.

'Oh, she really was, she lent me the money straightaway and yes, she was always lovely whenever we met her,' Kimmy blabbered.

Claire, who I knew by now was a little more astute, responded differently. 'I bet you're wondering how someone can be so nice when she's had two affairs in just over a year?'

That was one of a number of things puzzling me about Cherry. ' I just want to get a picture of what she's like, so I can help the police figure out who killed her.'

'I think she was young and naïve, and genuinely loved Pedro,' Claire continued. 'I didn't get it at first, especially with her age. I mean, it looked like the classic gold-digger story at first. Waitress in his restaurant has an affair with the owner twice her age, she must be after all of his money. But it wasn't like that, she didn't need his money, not that he had any.'

This was another puzzle. 'Why was she working part-time as a waitress if she didn't need the money?'

'Independence. She wanted to live her own life away from her family. She's been doing a Business degree at Brighton University and wanted to strike out on her own while she was studying. Apparently they used to bring her to Chalk Gap as a child and she fell in love with it, so she decided to move here.'

'It's quite sad really,' Kimmy added. 'From what we could tell, her family were rich but I'm not sure how happy a life she had with them. Her dad died when she was young and I think her Mum struggled after that. I think Cherry saw Pedro as a father figure.'

There were still pieces of this story missing though. 'And then she found another father figure in the Reverend?'

'I guess so, that's what puzzled us too. We grew to like her and she seemed like a nice girl, but like I said, how can she be nice with these two affairs? Kimmy and I have talked about it a lot. But all these goings-ons in the last year or so – Pedro and

Cherry, Reverend Flowers and Cherry, Gloria's antics, now these two murders – we're starting to think you never know your friends for real, only what they show you.'

That reminded me of something else. 'Oh, Everest Brown is staying with you isn't he? What do you know about him? Mum told me you only get a place on the winter market if you're close with the Vicar, so who is he? He said out there that he has family in the village.'

The two exchanged a look again. 'You're so funny, Edward, you ask all the same questions we did,' Kimmy said, having cheered up a little.

'Yes, we've wondered about that a lot,' Claire chipped in. 'Reverend Flowers brought him to the village, he asked us if we could put him up at the B&B for the couple of months he was here for the market.'

' And he had Christmas day with the Flowers family,' Kimmy said.

'So we think his family must be the Flowers in some capacity, but we can't work out why it's all so secretive.'

And now Frances is dead, and we still don't know his connection to them, I thought. While the Flowers family were on my mind, I remembered something else I wanted to ask. 'Pedro told Jacob Flowers he was fired this morning, he worked at the restaurant?'

'That's right,' Claire confirmed. 'For the last year or two. His Dad wanted him to have a job outside of the family, and we don't have enough for him to do here. He did quit for a while when the whole Pedro and Cherry thing first happened, I guess in solidarity with Gloria, but somehow they sorted it out between them that he went back.'

'He likes working there and Pedro says he's good at his job, so it was a good arrangement for everyone,' Kimmy said.

I thanked them both, told Kimmy not to worry and led them back into the church hall. Before I rejoined PC Wood, I wanted a few minutes to think and process everything.

Despite the new information, I still didn't feel like I quite had all the pieces. In fact, I had more questions than answers. But I knew where some of those answers might lie – on Cherry's phone.

23

'I'm sorry, mate, the phone's dead. A quick boost will do the trick though, I've got a charger on me.'

This wasn't what I wanted to hear from PC Wood. He insisted it would only take a minute to get some charge, but I'd rather be free to look at the messages on there in detail, particularly in light of Kimmy's confession.

I decided to give it half an hour and use the time to try Reverend Flowers again; technically, he and Jacob should have been under supervision until the police arrived, like everyone else.

As I clambered down the path from the hall to the church itself, the snow was still thick and difficult to walk through, but it had stopped falling at least. Part of me hoped that the police would be here soon to take this case off my hands, but the other part of me wanted to get to the bottom of this myself.

As I neared the church, I saw Flowers come out of it, slam the large wooden door shut and head in the opposite direction to me towards the Vicarage house. I don't know why, but something stopped me from calling out to him (even though I wanted to speak to him); I decided to hang back and follow behind him instead.

He reached the door and fumbled with his keys, as I ducked into the ginnel that led to the back of the Vicarage, out of sight but close enough to hear him rustling around with the key. I jumped a little when I suddenly heard him speak, but I soon realised that he was talking to his son at the doorway.

'Where are you going? You can't just keep storming away, Jacob, we need to talk.'

'Shut up, I've nothing to say to you. How could you do this to me, Dad?'

There was a silence for a moment. 'You don't think I did this, how could you?'

'No, I don't mean the murders, idiot.'

'I'll forgive that under the circumstances, Jacob.'

'Oh you're good at that, aren't you? Forgiveness? Well, are you going to forgive me?' I could hear his voice raising almost to a shout.

'For what?'

'Oh, plenty of things. But I'll add this to the list.'

I heard a commotion and a shout, and peaked out from the alley to see Reverend Flowers laying in the snow, with Jacob stood over him. I remained where I was, listening, but I was ready to move if Jacob tried to attack his father any more than the push.

'How could you betray me like that Dad? And Mum too. You ruined everything. You caused it, it's your fault. I'll never forgive you. I hate you.'

There was a few seconds of silence, before I heard trudging in the snow and then the Reverend's voice. 'Jacob. We can sort this out, I promise you. I know you loved her, Jacob. I know you loved her.'

There was no noise now and I could tell Jacob had gone. I waited a few moments and then revealed myself. 'Reverend Flowers, let me help you up.'

'Edward, thank you. How much of that did you hear?'

'A little,' I answered, as diplomatically as I could.

'He's just struggling with his mother's death.'

'Naturally,' I reassured him.

'Anyway, I owe you an apology for earlier, Edward. I was quite rude. I'll of course come along with you now. I'm not sure where Jacob will get to, though. Do you think the police will make do with me, once they get here? He's very upset about his mother.'

I told him that I expected they'd need to speak to Jacob as soon as they started the formal interviews, especially as he was 18 and not a minor. I expected the Reverend to complain or kick up a fuss, but he didn't. He just trundled alongside me to the church hall, deep in thought.

24

It was interesting watching Reverend Flowers arrive at the church hall and how it affected the dynamics of the others already sitting there.

Pedro immediately jumped up and away from Claire and Kimmy, instead sitting with my mum. Everest gave the Vicar a polite, sympathetic nod you'd expect to a grieving neighbour or colleague you know a little. There was nothing to suggest a particularly familiar relationship between them.

Where I did see a familiar relationship, or rather an over familiar one, was with Gloria. She leapt out of her seat and ran to hug the Reverend before taking his hand to lead him to sit with her.

'Don't worry about anything, we can sort it out,' I heard her whisper to him. She had some front, I'd give her that much.

'The phone's charged enough, mate,' PC Wood called out to me as the Reverend sat down. I took it from him and headed to the small room to read it in private, though maybe not that private as I noticed Noah follow me.

'I don't get to look at the phone with you?'

Wood said after me, sounding disappointed.

'You're the only police officer here, we need you to oversee the suspects. The murderer is almost certainly among them, so we need you: guarding a killer is a big responsibility. I'm sure it's the role DI Appleby would give you.'

'Of course, mate, leave it with me.' He said as he stood proudly. I thought he might even salute me.

'I'm so excited we get to examine a piece of evidence!' Noah said with glee as soon as we got into the other room. 'I was getting a bit bored keeping an eye on the suspects with PC Wood. I know he's a policeman, but he doesn't have a mind for investigations like we do. I kept telling him all my theories but he didn't seem to understand them.'

I resisted chuckling to myself at the meeting of the minds that was Noah and PC Wood as I went into the phone. It was an IPhone, but a quite older, smaller model like an IPhone 5 or 6. I'd have thought Cherry may have had the newest version, but Kimmy and Claire had already suggested she was quite modest with money.

The first thing I went to check was the messages with Kimmy about the borrowed money. My brain works in a quite logical way, so rather than look for any juicier evidence of the affair, I wanted to see the messages I'd been told about.

Except they weren't there.

'You need to check WhatsApp, Facebook Messenger and Instagram messages, not just normal text messages,' Noah said when I explained to him. I do have a WhatsApp group with Patrick, Kat, Alfie and Dylan but I wouldn't have thought to check all the various forms of social media like Noah did, so I was glad to have him there.

Except Kimmy's messages still weren't there. Maybe Cherry had deleted them to protect Kimmy's privacy.

Next, I looked at Cherry's messages with Pedro. They were fairly regular, seemed happy and couple-ish enough, though in the last couple of weeks there weren't quite as many. The only message that indicated any trouble in their marriage was one sent by Pedro last night:

9:23PM, PEDRO TO CHERRY: Cherry, my love, I'm sorry I don't want to kick you out. Please come back. I will forgive you. I love you baby xxxxx

It was an IMessage between Apple phones and I could see it remained unread 'til just now. There were also several missed calls from Pedro around that time and afterwards for the rest of the evening.

Finally, I looked at the messages with the only other recipient of her texts. The person was saved with several flower emojis instead of their name, though it only took me to read a few of them to identify them as between Cherry and Reverend

Flowers, and that they were having an affair. However, it was the messages sent last night that particularly interested me.

7:12PM, CHERRY TO FLOWERS: Pedro knows. Talking now. Will message xx

7:54PM, CHERRY TO FLOWERS: He's kicking me out. Can I come to you? xx

7:59PM, CHERRY TO FLOWERS: Hello? Xx

8:11PM, CHERRY TO FLOWERS: I'm on my way to Vicarage xx

8:14PM, CHERRY TO FLOWERS: Sneak out and meet me at bottom of West Chalk Cliff, at back of pub xx

8:15PM, CHERRY TO FLOWERS: It's snowing quite heavy though, will be there ASAP. 8.30? xx

8:23PM, FLOWERS TO CHERRY: Can't meet now. Don't come. Go somewhere else, will call tomorrow x

8:25PM, CHERRY TO FLOWERS: What? I'm nearly there. Come meet me xxx

8:32PM, CHERRY TO FLOWERS: I'm here. Come out xx

8:35PM, CHERRY TO FLOWERS: Come now or I'm coming to the Vicarage x

8:35PM, CHERRY TO FLOWERS: I mean it.

That was the last message in her phone. I showed them to Noah and he read them through too. 'The place she wanted to meet is right where you found the body.'

I'd realised this immediately. 'But it doesn't mean he was the one to meet her there.'

'Of course not,' Noah replied. 'Pedro could have followed her and been the one to kill her, then sent a fake text afterwards to cover his back.'

Again, this had occurred to me too. 'But Pedro couldn't have killed Frances, he has an alibi. And we don't know the full crime scene details yet, or even when Cherry died.'

'But Reverend Flowers could have killed Frances.' He thought for a moment. 'I know I keep talking about a big plot twist but sometimes there isn't one. Sometimes it is just the obvious person.'

I didn't know, something still didn't feel quite right. But I didn't get much chance to say anything further.

'Edward, mate, I made it! The snow plough is almost through, but I got through the last bit on foot.' DI Appleby was covered in snow almost from head to toe, and looked both freezing and tired. But he had a big grin on his face; he was thrilled to get through and join the action. 'What's the latest then? Wood told me you're looking at the phone. Any evidence?'

I passed him the phone and he read the chain of messages quietly. When he finished, he looked up with determination on his face. 'I think this is pretty clear, mate, don't you?'

'It seems it,' I conceded. 'We need to talk to Reverend Flowers.'

'Talk to him?' Appleby scoffed. 'I need to arrest him.'

'No,' I disagreed. 'I think you should question him first without arresting him, to see what he says.'

We heard a noise behind us and turned to see Reverend Flowers in the open doorway, with PC Wood behind him. 'I tried to stop him bursting in, he wouldn't listen.'

'Sorry to interrupt, gentlemen. Thank you for trying to defend me, Edward, but I think we all know what needs to happen.' He looked straight at Appleby. 'I am confessing to the murders of my wife, Frances Flowers, and my mistress, Cherry McDonald. I will make a full formal confession on arrest.'

'Very well,' Appleby said as he stepped forward. 'PC Wood, handcuff him please. Reverend Allan Flowers, you are under arrest on suspicion of the murders of Frances Flowers and Cherry McDonald. You do not have to say anything, but it may harm your defence if you do not mention when questioned something you later rely on in court. Anything you do say may be given in evidence.'

Flowers didn't speak again, he just calmly nodded his head. I watched in disbelief as they led him out of the room in handcuffs.

25

'I told you, didn't I, Edward? It's always the husband.'

'Yes, Mum, I suppose you did,' I replied through a deep sigh. It was about 20 minutes after Reverend Flowers had been taken away following his confession, and we were all sitting in the pub: my family (including Noah and Dylan), Patrick, Becky and Kat, who was finally having a rest after all her hard work co-ordinating the snowstorm volunteers. After the shock we'd all had, Mum had even let Gloria back into the pub, although I noticed she was alone, whilst Kimmy, Claire, Pedro and Everest all had a table together. Pedro looked broken.

The rest of Appleby's team had made it through shortly after he did, and Chalk Gap Road was finally clear for access in and out of the village. My part in the investigation was officially over: they had a confession, and now the police professionals could access the crime scenes properly, and get all the evidence they needed to hand over to the Crown Prosecution Service.

'Let's not forget the work our Edward did once

again,' Dad declared as he raised his glass. 'I know the killer confessed, but it's all thanks to our son's hard work investigating, finding those messages on the phone.'

'Anyone can read text messages on a phone, Dad,' I said back to him, snapping slightly. I didn't mean to, but I didn't feel quite right. Things hadn't happened how I'd expected them to, and it was affecting me. I wasn't sure if it was the sense of anti-climax that a confession had ended my investigation, rather than me unmasking the murderer. Secretly, I'd enjoyed (though that feels like the wrong word when there are deaths involved) the sense of achievement in solving a murder previously; it's no secret that anxiety has stopped me from achieving many of my goals, and this had given me a bigger sense of purpose than I'd ever had as a school librarian.

'No, buddy, your dad's right,' Patrick said. 'The police couldn't get through, and you stepped up and did their jobs for them.'

'We're all proud of you,' Alfie added.

'Course we are,' Mum chipped in. 'And Noah too.' He beamed at this.

'Thanks, everyone,' I managed. They all meant well, and they always had my back.

'I just can't believe it's Reverend Flowers,' Kat said. 'He was always so nice, whenever he did fundraising with the school. And his position too.

Oh, and his poor son. What will happen to him? I wonder if the school can help somehow.'

'He's 18 though,' Patrick pointed out. 'I'm not sure if that will make a difference.'

'Yes, it might do,' Kat agreed. 'I'll speak to one of the police officers in a moment and find out what's happening to him.'

'I've not even seen him around since, poor kid,' Mum said. 'His dad killing his mum and his mistress, he won't know what to think.'

'You'd think you'd have to be a good person to be a Vicar,' Becky said with her hand in Patrick's.

'He was a good person, he was a decent bloke,' Dad said.

'I'm not so sure, love,' Mum chipped in. 'I never trusted him.'

'Come on, love,' Dad said to her. 'He was, you just didn't like him because you could never get in with that group and the market stuff.'

'Yes, it is odd, with his group of women always round him,' Dylan said.

'He liked controlling them all,' Mum said, determined to be right.

'There was more to that group than meets the eye,' I replied to her.

Yes, I understood how Flowers could be viewed as controlling, and had even glimpsed it myself.

His relationship with his wife certainly had question marks around it, even without the affair; leaving her alone after the fight whilst taking the other ladies to the Vicarage was very odd. And the affair itself, which we had mobile phone evidence of, didn't suggest a good Christian man.

And finally, of course, he'd confessed to the murder. That should have been case closed. But something didn't sit right. I remembered how Reverend Flowers acted on his doorstep, and how pensive he was walking back to the church hall. And when he confessed, I couldn't put my finger on it, but there was something that just didn't sit right. And then something dawned on me.

'Are you okay, son?' I heard Dad asking. I realised I'd not spoken for a good minute, deep in my thoughts.

'No, not really,' I found myself replying, still in a daze. I started to stand up. 'Noah, can you come with me please?'

'Yes, of course! But where?'

'Edward, what's going on?' Mum asked, looking confused, as did everyone at the table.

'Noah and I have work to do,' I said in reply. 'I don't think Reverend Flowers did it.'

'But he confessed,' Dad pointed out.

'I know he did, but I think he's innocent. The Reverend didn't murder anyone, and I'm going to prove it.'

26

'*The wrong culprit* twist, what a shocker!' Noah said as he followed me through the snow across the square. 'I should have realised that wasn't the end of the story. There's no way the murderer just confesses and that's it. The detectives have to reveal the real murderer, that's how it works!'

Okay, so my declaration in the pub was perhaps a tad dramatic, and it had resulted in Noah following suit by getting over excited about all his murder mystery stuff, with us as the triumphant detectives. But I had a strong determination to clear the Reverend's name and reveal the real culprit. Looking back, it seemed strange that I knew as strongly as I did there was more to the story, as I wasn't even sure of the facts when I said that. I just knew it wasn't as simple as Flowers' confession. I just knew it.

'Where are we going, anyway?' Noah enquired as he struggled to keep up with me. 'Most people we need to speak to are in the pub.'

'One person isn't,' I replied as I reached where I wanted to go and called out the name of who I needed to speak to. 'PC Wood.'

'Hello, mate,' the young policeman said, as he broke himself away from his colleagues at Cherry's crime scene. 'Everything's getting sorted now, I'm glad we've got back-up to do everything officially.' He smiled sadly. 'Mind you, it seems a bit of a shame everyone else is here now, I enjoyed doing our bit.'

'So did I,' Noah said with his typical enthusiasm. 'But it's not over yet.'

What's he talking about?' Wood asked, looking puzzled.

'I need your help with a few things,' I said, looking round to check his colleagues were out of hearing distance. 'But I need you to keep it between us for now, not to tell DI Appleby.'

'Oh, I don't know about that,' he replied, looking nervous. 'I'm not in the habit of doing things like that.'

I'd started to like Dean Wood. He was naïve, got things wrong and still had a lot to learn, but he was a good, honest, loyal policeman. Which was why I knew he'd be the right person to help. 'Look, DI Appleby asked me to help originally because he trusts me. And I need you to do the same. I need you to trust me. I think there's a murderer still out there, but if Appleby's going to believe my theory, I need to get the evidence I need first. Which is where I want your help.'

He considered me for a moment with a worried

expression on his face. Then he spoke. 'Yeah, go on then, mate. I'll do it. I'll help you. What do you need?'

'I'll explain, but let's walk this way a bit,' I said, guiding him back towards the main square, away from his colleagues. 'You helped secure both crime scenes, didn't you?'

'Yes, mate,' he replied proudly. 'Remember, I told you, I felt like I was finally getting to do proper police work.'

'And you gave me Cherry's mobile phone from the second crime scene,' I added. 'But I wanted to know, do you know what happened to Frances Flowers' mobile phone from the first crime scene?'

'It's funny you should say that, we were just talking about it,' he started in response. 'We just thought Mrs Flowers didn't have it on her person at the time like Cherry did, but now they've searched the whole Vicarage and they still can't find it.'

'Missing evidence!' Noah declared, waving his gloved hands in the air.

'What are the theories on it?' I asked.

'DC Gillespie from CID reckons that the Reverend must have hidden it or got rid of it, back when he wasn't going to confess,' Wood replied. 'She thinks it must have contained some evidence against him.'

'Oh yes?' I prompted.

'Yeah, and DC Bowie says DI Appleby will have to ask Flowers what he's done with it. Even though he's confessed, they'll still want all the evidence they can. These CID guys, though. They think they know everything.'

'And what do you think, Dean?'

'I dunno,' he mused, deep in thought. 'I guess they're husband and wife, they live together, and we already know he was having a conversation with her right before the time of her death. So, I don't really see what evidence would be on the phone, and why he would have needed to hide it. Unless it was to hide evidence of the affair.'

'Why did he leave Cherry's phone on her person then?' I countered.

'I don't know, mate, but that's not the only strange thing, now you mention it.'

'Go on?' I said. I'd been unsure of this tactic, of trying to get information from PC Wood, but it seemed to be paying fruit.

'At Frances' crime scene, I find the footprints in the snow a bit odd,' he said.

'Oh yes, the footprints!' Noah said in delight. He loved tangible evidence. 'We think the murderer must have escaped over the fence to the cliff bottoms at the other side.'

I wasn't sure of his use of 'we' there; I didn't

necessarily think this myself. 'But now that makes no sense, Noah. Why would Reverend Flowers do that? He wouldn't need to escape. He could just simply go back into his own house.'

'Oh yes,' Noah replied. 'Maybe the footprints are our red herring; maybe they were there from earlier in the morning by one of the family naturally, and they're nothing to do with the murder.'

'No, that's unlikely,' PC Wood said back. 'The snow was already falling then, they can't have been from too long before or else we wouldn't have seen them. They were already half covered up when we got to them.'

'That's a really good point, Dean,' I said, impressed. 'What do you think then?'

'Well, actually, I have something interesting to show you,' he said, taking his phone out of his pocket and loading a photo up. 'Look at this footprint I took a picture of, when I was helping with the crime scene. You can only just make it out as the snow's started to cover it, but look closely at the print. You can see it facing towards the fence fairly clearly, but look when I zoom in. The footprint also very faintly points the other way, heading back towards the house.'

'It could be that they came via the back fence, and then went back that way,' Noah suggested.

'Possibly,' Wood replied, 'but it seems so faint that it seems like they were trying not to even leave a print. Suggesting they wanted us to see the print going to the fence, but not back again.'

'That's a really good theory,' I added, pleased that we had a development. 'And adding to that, I checked with both Kat and Appleby about the house to house stuff they were co-ordinating, and everyone we've accounted for sledging on the cliffside didn't see anyone at all. Which is odd if we're saying they climbed over the fence twice.'

'If we're going with the theory that it wasn't Reverend Flowers but someone else, they must have really escaped back through the house then,' Noah said. The three of us seemed to be working well together.

'Think about it,' Wood said quickly in excitement. 'You've just committed a murder, you've used footprints to cause confusion. You're not going to use your own shoes for that. So, you bring another pair with you. But you have to get rid of them soon after. You don't want them found so you can't throw them away too near the scene, but at the same time you don't want anyone to recall seeing you with a conspicuous looking object. So what do you do with them?'

I was really glad of PC Wood at that moment; his logical, simple approach to evidence was exactly what we needed. 'You put them somewhere away from the Vicarage, but as quickly as you can, and where no one will think to look. The only thing is, I can't think where.'

'I think I might know somewhere,' I said, an idea forming in my head. 'Come with me.'

27

We were just across the village square, at the re-cycling area, which housed several large recycling bins of every item you could imagine, including bins for unwanted clothes and shoes.

'The murderer may not have took the time to deposit the shoes in the correct bin,' I mused to my two helpers, 'but it's as good a place to start as any. If we can get in there, that is.'

The shoes bin had a one way chute to deposit items, which made it difficult to look what was in there.

'That's easy,' Noah said. 'We know that if our shoes are in here, they'll be at the top if they were only deposited a few hours ago. If we're lucky, the bin is full so it won't be far to reach. I'm the small-est, you two lift me up and I'll see what I can find.'

'Brilliant, mate!' PC Wood replied. 'Come on then.'

Who knows what we must have looked like, there at the recycling bins, in the snow, with us lifting Noah high enough so he could rummage round in the shoe bin.

'This is so exciting!' Noah said, as I struggled to hold his weight. 'I think that's what our mysteries have been lacking, some action scenes: us chasing round for clues, things like that.'

PC Wood looked at me in bewilderment. 'Don't even ask,' I mouthed as quietly as I could.

'Hang on, got something!' Noah announced loudly from above us. 'It's in a bag, hang on... got it!' He pulled out a bright coloured bag as we lifted him back down to the snow-covered ground.

The first thing I noticed was the paper bag the shoes were in: it was a red and white striped large paper bag, and I recognised it from earlier that day as the largest size of Gloria's sweets bags, and told my two helpers this.

'Oh, so does that mean it could be her?' PC Wood asked.

'Don't assume anything yet,' I told him. I'd learned that already from everything so far in this case.

'And she had an alibi for the first murder,' Noah added. 'Anyway, let's look in the bag!'

We opened it to find a pair of plain black Converse style trainers, covered in snow. PC Wood looked closely to find out the size. 'They're size 8s. They could be anyone's.'

'We need to ask all the suspects their shoe size!' Noah said with glee.

'I dunno, boys,' PC Wood said. 'This is evidence, I should maybe hand them straight over to Appleby.'

'Yes, you probably should,' I agreed. 'But I have an idea. Can you just let me take them somewhere first, and then I'll bring them back for you to give to Appleby? I think I know where they might be from.'

28

The trek up the cliffside wasn't quite as difficult as when I'd pursued Jacob earlier, now that the snow had stopped falling. But it was still a massive challenge in the still thick snow, particularly for someone uncoordinated and not particularly fit like me.

It was worth it, though; there sitting at the top, when I eventually got there, was Jacob. 'Edward, what are you doing here?' He hadn't shouted at me to go away, which seemed to be progress from what I'd seen so far today of this angry young man.

'I guessed you'd be here,' I replied. 'I wanted to talk to you and check you're okay.'

'I'm impressed, I suppose,' he grunted. 'I've been coming up here to get away for years, my parents never found me. Only stupid Auntie Gloria, but she thinks she knows everything. Not that either of my parents can find me now.'

He clocked my reaction and spoke again. 'Yes, I know about my dad confessing to the murder. I do have a mobile phone, you know. Must have had twenty different kids text me about it. Even the ones who don't even bother saying hello to me.'

I wanted to talk about this further but I knew it would be an emotional conversation, so I wanted to ask him my question first. 'I need to show you something, Jacob, and then ask you a question.'

I hadn't brought the trainers with me; I could barely climb up there as it was, without carrying a bag too. I showed him the photos of them I'd taken on my phone. 'Do you recognise these trainers, Jacob?'

'Let me see,' he said with some interest, until his expression changed. 'Wait, yeah, they're mine! Oi, where did you get them? They're my trainers I wear for work. I... I haven't seen them for ages though.'

'It's fine, they're not important,' I lied. 'We found them and Noah thought he recognised them as yours. I just thought I'd ask you while I was here.'

'Yeah, alright, just give me them back sometime. Not like I've got a job to wear them for now anyway.'

Out of all the things he'd lost today, it appeared surprising that his job was the one he was focusing on. But I had a theory, one I was almost sure of, that might explain that.

'Jacob, I need to ask you a personal question. Before you get angry, I want to say you don't have to answer it if you don't want to, but if you do, it would really help me and I think it might help your dad too.'

'Go on,' he said, eyeing me suspiciously.

'It isn't an easy question, but here it is. When you got angry at Noah this morning, you said Cherry's name first, and then your dad's after, do you remember?'

He answered quickly and sharply, without hesitation. 'Yeah, so?'

'And I'm really sorry, but I was coming to see your dad before, I accidentally overheard your argument with him.'

He looked down at the snow, ashamed. 'I didn't mean to push him like that.'

'I know, don't worry. He was fine afterwards and I think it's forgivable under the circumstances.'

'Ah, good old forgiveness,' he retorted. 'It's all Dad talks about – forgive this, forgive that.'

'Anyway,' I said, keen to move on to what I wanted to say, 'I heard your Dad say to you, "I know you loved her." At first, I thought he was talking about your mum, and of course you loved your mum. But he wasn't talking about her, was he?'

I knew I was potentially on thin ice with this volatile teenager, but when I saw the tear in his eye, I knew I was right.

'Jacob, he was talking about Cherry, wasn't he? You were in love with her.'

29

I rounded up the conversation with Jacob fairly swiftly after that. I'd treaded very carefully on purpose, ensuring I didn't anger him or accuse him of anything. I'd found out what I needed to know for now: that the trainers belonged to Jacob, that he himself was in love with Cherry, and that his father had realised this.

I was starting to form a theory, and I was almost ready to present it to Appleby. But not quite. I wanted to have two conversations first, for my own peace of mind: one directly linked to the solution of the case, the other a little more personal one.

I was lucky enough to find the first person I needed to speak to as I arrived back in the square, after nearly breaking my neck a hundred times coming down the snow-filled cliff slope.

Everest Brown was in his *Burger She Wrote* van sorting out stock when I arrived to speak to him.

'I'm not really open,' he said, 'but I can do you a quick vegan burger I reckon.'

'No, it's okay, I wanted a chat with you actually,' I explained.

'Oh sorry, man, I just realised you're the po-lice helper investigator guy! Yeah, I'm glad you've found me, I was gonna have a chat with you, actu-ally.'

This was interesting, but if I was right, I thought I knew what about. 'Yes, I'm Edward, pleased to meet you properly. You were really shocked Rev-erend Flowers confessed to the murders, weren't you?'

'As a matter of fact, Edward, yes I was. Allan Flowers is a good guy, one of the best. He's helped me out so much. It might be too late and it prob-ably won't mean much, but I don't think he did it, I don't see how he could have, he's not a killer.'

'I agree with you, and it's one of the reasons I wanted to speak to you.' I continued, preparing for the important question. 'But there's another reason too. You said you have family in the village. You came here to find your son, didn't you?'

I saw the shock on his face; I knew he wasn't expecting me to say that. He thought for a second, then grinned. 'There's no use denying it, if you've got as far as working that out. You're really good at this investigation stuff, aren't you?'

I blushed at the compliment and pressed on. 'My guess is, you got in touch with the local Rev-erend to help establish yourself in our little close-knit village. You probably told him you needed help reuniting with family, but I don't think you told him who. He agreed to set you up on the winter market, and you've been settling in the village since, waiting for the chance to reveal who you are.'

Wow, man. How do you know all this?' He seemed genuinely amazed, but I'd just used logic.

'Reverend Flowers has been getting criticism for having his favourites, but I've learned he's a man who will always help those in need. He does so much fundraising with the school I work at, for example. But I also know he's protective over his market, and most people there have a connection with him. When I learned you had family in the village but wouldn't say who, I just pieced the rest together.'

'But how did you know it was a son?'

I looked at him and spoke gently. 'because I know who it is. And I know he needs you.'

30

The second conversation I wanted to have was with someone I knew much better. I'd sent a text, asking him to meet me privately in the church hall.

'Edward, buddy!' Patrick said warmly as he arrived. 'What's up?'

'Come sit down,' I said, pointing to a chair. 'Thanks for coming so quickly, I want to have a chat.'

'Sure, buddy, anything. Do you need help with your investigation?'

'Kind of. This will seem quite strange, seeing as last time you saw me, I was rushing off to prove Reverend Flowers' innocence. But I actually don't want to talk about that. I wanted to ask about you and Becky, and Kat. Is everything okay?'

He looked puzzled, which seemed to the reaction I was evoking in all of the last few people I'd spoken to. 'Do you mean what I said this morning about Kat, and why she moved out? Yeah, that's all fine, I was being silly.'

'Yes, partly that, and also when we were all in

the pub the first time today, you reacted strangely around Kat a couple of times. You seemed jealous when she mentioned Appleby, for example.'

'Wow, Edward, I hope Becky isn't a good a detective as you,' he said, laughing nervously. 'If it was anyone else, I'd worry I was being too obvious.'

'Do you still have feelings for Kat?'

'No, at least I don't think so. It's a strange one, buddy. I really like Becky, she's a great girl and it's going very well. But a lot of things are changing all at once. Kat moving out, me moving on. It just makes me a little sad, that's all. When all three of us were single in that house, there was always the possibility we could get back together. And that's not there anymore.'

'Is that a bad thing?' I asked.

'I thought it was, but I've realised I'm being silly. Me and Kat belong in the past as a couple, we're exes for a reason. But Becky could be the future. Or maybe not, but I still have to take the risk and go for it. Two women have died today, one ten years younger than us. If that's not a message to seize the day, I'm not sure what is.'

I reflected on what he said and then asked my next question. 'Do you think some part of you will always love Kat?'

He didn't hesitate. 'Yes, buddy, of course. Not in

love with her, but you know, she was such a big part of my life when we were together, and still is now. That doesn't go away, especially when we're still so close.'

'I suppose it's unusual, you two staying best friends,' I mused. 'I guess it's more common for exes to hate each other, like Gloria and Pedro do.'

'I don't get that though, Edward. I suppose our village is small and you can't avoid each other, but if you can't stay friends like us, you should avoid each other completely. Not have big dramatic public rows like they always do.'

'I guess so,' I agreed. 'I'm glad you and Kat didn't end up like that.'

'We never would. Anyway, thanks for checking on me, but enough about that. How about you, you think you're found the real killer then?'

I reflected on all the new things I'd had con-firmed that afternoon, piecing it together with all the other information I'd acquired through the day. 'You know what, Patrick? I think I have.'

31

As Patrick and I returned to the pub, DI Appleby burst out of the doors towards us, with a sheepish PC Wood in tow. 'Edward, mate, what have you been up to?'

'What do you mean?' I asked, though I had an idea what he meant.

'I came looking for you, but it's chaos in there. They're all saying you're trying to prove it's not Reverend Flowers, even though he confessed. That Pedro guy is going ballistic.' He exhaled strongly, clearly stressed. 'Anyway, I managed to get it out of PC Wood here, that you are snooping round after all.'

'Appleby, I'm sorry.' I braced myself and continued. 'Yes, I have been looking into it, and the Reverend didn't do it. And I can prove it.'

'What?' he replied. 'Look, mate, you know I'm grateful for all your help, but your part is done now. We've got a culprit, who's happily confessed to both murders. Even though he was the pretty obvious suspect before that anyway.'

'Yes, he was obvious. We were supposed to

think it's obvious. Let me explain.'

We heard a commotion inside the pub. 'Edward, you've helped me out and I trust you. So, for that reason, I'll hear you out. But first, let's go smooth over whatever's happening in there.'

The four of us walked in to find Pedro and Gloria both stood up in the centre of the pub, verbally facing off against each other. They hadn't noticed us yet.

'Of course you're mad that Edward is saying it's not the Reverend! You're worried he'll find out it was you, not him.'

'If I was capable of killing a woman,' he shouted back, 'you'd have been top of my list, not them!'

'A threat, that's a threat to kill me! You all heard that!' she yelled around the room dramatically.

And then Pedro spotted me. 'Edward, you were supposed to be my friend! But we have the killer of my beloved Cherry, and you are trying to set him free! Why would you disrespect her memory like that?'

I was reluctant to join the floor show, but I found myself speaking. 'I'm not trying to disrespect Cherry's memory, Pedro. I just know that Reverend Flowers didn't kill her, or his wife.'

'Be careful, mate,' Appleby whispered to me.

'Yes he did,' Pedro said firmly.

'No he didn't,' I replied, trying to sound just as firm. 'And as soon as we leave here, I'm going to explain it all to DI Appleby.'

'Oh, never mind that,' Mum piped up. 'Tell us all here, in the pub.'

'He's not going to do that,' Appleby said back to her.

I looked around the room. All of the suspects were here, the police, plus Noah, my family and my friends. Even Jacob Flowers was skulking at a table on his own in the background. I think I got a little carried away imagining the triumphant end scene, where the detective cleverly reveals whodunnit and how it was done. Before I knew it, I was replying to Appleby in a private whisper.

'You know what, I think I should.'

'What? Have you lost your mind, mate?' he whispered back.

'Everyone I need is here, I have a water tight case, and I can prove it. But if you haven't seen enough to convince you at the end, you can walk away with nothing to do with it. It was just the geeky amateur poking his nose in again.'

He thought for a moment and then rolled his eyes. 'Fine, mate, go for it then. I'm actually intrigued. But remember, this is nothing to do with me.'

'What are you two whispering about?' Mum

complained across the pub. 'Edward, are you going to tell us what you know?'

'I'm going to do more than that, Mum. I'm going to prove that not only is the Reverend innocent, he was set up by someone in this room right now.'

'I'm so excited!' Noah declared, jumping up from his table. 'This is like a real life episode of *Poirot*! Edward, can I start things off, please?'

'But you don't know the solution to the case,' I pointed out.

'Yes, but I know the beginning of it. I'll just set the scene.' I noticed Jacob Flowers in the corner, watching us. I had a sudden realisation that this public reveal might not be fair to him. I walked over to his table while all eyes were on Noah. 'Jacob, I know the truth and I want to prove your dad didn't do it. But I don't have to do it like this if you don't want me to. I can talk to you privately.'

He looked at me, for once not revealing any particular emotion. 'No, go on, do it. I want to see what you come up with.' I nodded to Noah to start.

'Ladies and gentlemen, there have been several classic murder mysteries where the suspects were trapped in a snowstorm: *The Sittaford Mystery* and *Murder on the Orient Express* to name just two. And now I present to you, set in the little seaside village of Chalk Gap... *The Snow Day Murders*!'

'Do we really need all this drama?' Gloria asked, who had now taken a seat.

'Oh, be quiet, you,' Mum remarked. 'The drama's usually coming from you, it makes a change being someone else.'

'Over three feet of snow fell down on the village, probably more snow than Chalk Gap has ever seen,' Noah continued. 'No one can get in, no one can get out. A violent argument on the village square led the discovery of not one, but two bodies...'

'Yes, my friend, we know all this,' Pedro spoke now. 'Edward, if you say Reverend Flowers didn't kill my wife, you need to tell us now, please.'

'Yes, I'll get there,' I said, stepping forward, not as confidently as I'd have liked. 'Thank you Noah for setting the scene. I'm afraid I won't be quite as dramatic as Noah, I just want to tell you the facts: what they appear to be, and what they actually are.'

I was unsure where exactly to start when I heard Mum say to my dad, 'my money's on that vegan burger guy, if it's not the Vicar. Never trust a stranger, I say...'

This remark gave me inspiration on how to begin my explanation. 'I'll start with the newcomer to the village, Everest Brown.'

He nodded to me as I continued. 'Everest arrived in our village in November, in time for the start of our famous winter market, and has been here for the last two or three months since, with his vegan burger business *Burger She Wrote*. A few people speculated about his connection to Reverend Flowers, a stranger suddenly in a prominent position on the market, as everyone knows those spots are hard to come by. In fact, they usually only go to those closest to the Vicar.'

I stopped for a moment, suddenly hit by the realisation that I was speaking in public to a room full of people. But I also noticed that they all seemed to be listening intently. I continued. 'With that in mind, I asked myself, who is Everest Brown? What is his connection to Reverend Flowers? These unprecedented double murders occurred a couple of months after he arrived... could he be responsible?'

'Yes, course he is!' I heard Mum whisper.

'I'm afraid burgers are all she wrote, because Everest is not the murderer.' I paused again, having surprised myself with my showmanship. 'However, he was important as a witness to Reverend Flowers' good character. They didn't know each other until recently, but Everest got in touch with the Reverend to help him find someone in Chalk Gap, and Flowers helped him indeed, a huge amount, without even knowing the identity of who Everest was looking for. He came here to find a family member.'

'And who is it then?' Kimmy asked.

I looked at Everest's son listening intently, and then at Everest himself, who looked down. It wasn't time, and it wasn't fair for that revelation to be public. It had to be private.

'It's a personal matter for Everest I'm afraid,' I said, seeing the disappointment on Kimmy's face. But it was her own turn next, along with Claire. 'But you, Kimmy, and Claire too, have also been very important to the case. Connected to everyone involved as witnesses, friends and even alibis.'

I saw a nervous look on Kimmy's face as I continued. 'Claire and Kimmy were close friends with both of the murdered women, as well as with the Reverend, and the other suspects in the case. Kimmy came to me with a delicate matter; she confessed to texts on Cherry's phone which might implicate her in her murder.'

I saw the sudden interest in Gloria's face, as she looked at Kimmy with a smug grin, before muttering under her breath. 'Well, well, well.'

'But, even though Kimmy was worried about her secret, it was a secret not connected to the murder and one I won't be revealing here. Neither Kimmy or Claire are the murderers, and I want to thank Kimmy for being very honest with me. It actually helped me stumble on the real motive for the murders. Kimmy's messages weren't even on Cherry's phone when we found it, which was also a major clue.'

'Well done, baby,' I heard Claire say as the pair hugged in relief.

'However, I'm afraid Kimmy wasn't honest about everything she told me today, were you, Kimmy?'

I didn't enjoy the sudden panic I saw on Kimmy's face, and I felt a pang of guilt for doing this to her in this way. But it was a crucial part of the story. I reassured her. 'Kimmy, all I need you to do is just confirm there was something you lied about, but you were coaxed into it by someone else. It's okay, you were manipulated, but you did lie. You know what I'm talking about, don't you?'

Claire looked very confused, not knowing what was going on. Kimmy just nodded her head. 'Yes, I know what you're talking about, and yes, you're right.' I glanced at the person who made her lie to see their reaction, but they maintained a complete poker face.

Next, I turned to Jacob Flowers. But before I fully revealed his involvement in such a public way, I wanted to be sure he was okay with it. I looked at him tactfully, raising my eyebrows, mouthing, 'can I?'

He nodded. 'Yes, do it,' he mouthed back before I nodded my thanks.

'I'm not going to make a big dramatic show of

this next bit, as it's not fair to the person it involves. Jacob Flowers has been through so much and lost so much, today alone. But he's been heartbroken for a while, for a different reason. He's given me permission to share with you that he was in love with Cherry McDonald.'

I saw Pedro glare at him as everyone else looked stunned. Gloria was the first to speak. 'He's the killer then! He found out his Dad was having an affair with Cherry, so he killed her. Then he must have gone home in a rage, got into an argument with his mum, and killed her too.'

I panicked. I didn't want Gloria hi-jacking my explanation, and I didn't want to put Jacob through too much. But she wasn't finished. 'Oh my god... that's why Reverend Flowers confessed! He realised his son committed both murders, and he falsely confessed himself to protect him.'

There was a murmur round the pub as Gloria's words sank in. I could see everyone realise that this could be the truth.

'Oh my god, mate, is that what happened?' Appleby asked me quietly from where he stood near me.

The pub was chaos now; I wasn't expecting Gloria to derail my plans like this. I noticed PC Wood stood to attention, ready to make an arrest. I had to do something.

'I wasn't going to reveal that like this,' I confessed. 'And I'm sorry, Jacob. But, yes, Reverend Flowers confessed to the murders to protect his son. The Reverend didn't do it.'

'So he did!' Pedro shouted as he stood up, looking ready to attack.

'It's a very plausible explanation,' I said. 'Reverend Flowers certainly thought his son was the killer. But that's because he was tricked into thinking so. Wasn't he, Gloria?'

32

'Whatever are you talking about, you stupid little man?' Gloria sneered at me from her table.

'Don't you talk to my son like that, unless you want another slap!'

Gloria stood up to face Mum with a look of absolute disdain on her face. 'Do you think I'm scared of you?'

'That's enough, thank you, ladies,' Appleby said, stepping forward. Both of them sat down.

I continued on. 'No, Gloria, you're probably not scared of my mum. I don't imagine you're scared of many people. You are a cold-blooded killer after all. You murdered your own friend, Frances Flowers.'

A hush fell over the whole pub and all eyes went to Gloria, who burst out laughing.

'I'm sorry, is this a joke?' She turned to DI Appleby and PC Wood. 'Are you going to allow this: some amateur, slandering innocent people with his little floor show, while the real killer is sitting across the pub from me?'

'I have a confession from the Reverend already,

it's done with, unless any new evidence comes to light soon.' He winked at me. 'For now, I'm just having a quick break, popping into my old local pub to say hello and watching the entertainment while I'm here. Edward hasn't broken any laws, so I can't do anything, I'm afraid.'

She looked absolutely furious, but also a little worried, as I continued.

'And you know all about floor shows, Gloria, but I'll come on to that.'

'Seriously, what is this idiot talking about?' she muttered to no one in particular, before returning to me. 'I can't have killed Frances anyway, I have an alibi. I was selling sweets and Kimmy Atkinson was helping me the whole time.'

Kimmy looked down at the floor as I went on. 'Except she wasn't, was she? You blackmailed Kimmy into giving you an alibi. You knew she had a secret because she came to you for help. And you also knew her wife didn't know, although she does now.' I saw Claire put her hand on Kimmy's.

'You turned her request down, but you used that knowledge for when you needed it. Which was when you needed a false alibi for Frances' murder.'

'What absolute rot,' Gloria said with venom in her voice.

'It isn't, it's true,' Kimmy said. 'She made me lie,

I'm sorry. If I need to go to prison, I will.'

'I don't think that will be necessary,' Appleby interjected. 'You haven't even given a formal statement yet, you've only had a chat with Edward.'

Kimmy looked relieved and hugged Claire, as Gloria spoke again. 'That doesn't mean anything, I just didn't want stupid Kimmy to know where I was going, that's all. I didn't kill anyone.'

'It's a shame that's not true, Gloria,' I said to her, my confidence rising now I knew I had Appleby's support. 'In fact, this whole crime isn't something you just planned today. No, you planned it a long time ago, starting with when got Jacob Flowers the job at *Pedro's*. It was very convenient for you that Jacob was going off the rails. It fitted perfectly to get him a job working with young, attractive, friendly Cherry. You knew his history and you knew what would likely happen. Sorry, Jacob.'

'It's okay,' he muttered. 'Carry on. If she's done it, say what you need to prove it.'

I thought Gloria was going to speak up again but she just glared at me in rage as I went on. 'You see, Jacob was part of a plot to frame the wrong person for the murders. But it wasn't just Reverend Flowers. She was cleverer than that. Her plan was arranged carefully enough that either the Reverend or Jacob himself could be set up to take the blame.'

'I've heard it all now, honestly -'

'Shut up, you murdering cow,' Mum snapped. 'This is getting good now, stop interrupting.'

I allowed myself a grin at Mum's comment. 'You thought it through so carefully. You planted Jacob's footprints at the crime scene at the Vicarage. If there wasn't enough evidence on the Reverend, his son's footprints were there to show him escaping over the fence and up the cliff side, something *Auntie Gloria* knew he did. You managed to get hold of his work trainers, though it will make sense how you got those in a moment. Anyway, you dumped his trainers in the recycling, which you didn't think we'd find.'

'Or otherwise you wouldn't have used a sweet shop bag,' Noah added proudly.

'But your main plan was to create the impression that Reverend Flowers was having an affair with Cherry, and your plan worked,' I continue, watching Jacob and Pedro's faces carefully.

'But to the Reverend himself, it was a different story. You spent the time telling him all about how his son was dangerously infatuated with Cherry. Once Pedro accused Flowers of the affair, everything you'd said made him think it must be his son. When I heard him on the phone to you, saying "Edward knows about the affair," he was actually talking about Jacob and Cherry. But there never was an affair, was there? Jacob had fallen hard for her, but Cherry genuinely loved Pedro. She didn't have an affair with anyone.'

'But how about Cherry's phone, though?' Noah asked. 'We saw the messages between Cherry and Reverend Flowers, they confirmed the affair.'

'Ah, the phones,' I said, settling into my role. 'Isn't it odd that Cherry's phone, found on her body, contained such important evidence, but Frances' phone was nowhere to be seen? Even an extensive police search of the house couldn't find it.'

'How on earth do you know that?' Appleby asked while Wood went bright red.

'The reason they couldn't find Frances' phone,' I continued, ignoring Appleby, 'was that it probably contained evidence revealing the *real* killer. If I had to guess, it probably contained a text from Gloria to Frances, asking to meet her at the back of the Vicarage to give her important information about the affair.'

'No, no, it didn't,' Gloria said, much weaker now, and I knew that's exactly what had happened.

'But Cherry's phone, found conveniently in her pocket, we were meant to find. For it told us oh so clearly about the affair: how Cherry had been kicked out by Pedro, how she asked to meet Flowers at the eventual scene of her murder, and how she threatened him when he didn't immediately go to meet her. But, in another clever touch, notice how I just said 'Flowers' and not the Reverend. Because this mysterious lover wasn't saved in the phone by name, he was saved as several flower emojis. And the messages were vague enough that they could have meant father or son, depending on who suspicion had fallen on.'

'So the messages were fake?' my dad asked.

'Yes, they were fake. It wasn't Cherry's phone, it was a dummy phone, planted to frame the wrong man and hide the real killer. Her real phone is of course nowhere to be found, and I doubt it's an old model like an Iphone 5. But, disturbingly, it wasn't just the messages last night on there, the fake phone had been used over many weeks to leave a whole history of false evidence.'

'But why?' PC Wood asked. 'I understand all that, but I don't understand why. Why would Gloria go to all this trouble to murder both women?'

'She didn't murder both women, she only murdered Frances. But she was very much the mastermind behind Cherry's murder.'

'Someone else killed Cherry then? I'm confused,' Wood said again.

'Yes, they did. I always thought Cherry's killer was likely a man; the strangle marks were from someone quite strong and bigger than her. I'd worked out how Gloria did Frances' murder, but I suspected she had a male accomplice. In fact, PC Wood, I thought it might have been you.'

Me?' he said incredulously.

'*The policeman did it* twist!' Noah shouted, clapping his hands together.

'It occurred to me that the snowstorm was a convenient time for the murders to happen, when the police couldn't get through. They'd have to rely on the local policeman for help, giving you the perfect opportunity you wouldn't have otherwise had to tamper with the crime scenes.'

'But I didn't do it!' he whined.

'Don't worry, I realised that very quickly,' I said as I smiled at him. 'In fact, you've been a brilliant help through the whole case, and a credit to the police force.' The young PC beamed with pride.

'So, who was her accomplice then?' Kimmy asked. 'There's no one else left. Only Pedro, and he and Gloria hate each other.'

'What makes you say they hate each other, Kimmy?' I asked.

She looked confused. 'Because we all know it. All the massive public rows, they even had one just now. They act like they hate each other.'

'Exactly,' I said. 'They *act* like they hate each other. But what if that's all it is, an act? A clever plot acted out over more than a year, all to get their hands on a fortune, murdering two innocent

people in the process? Because that's what happened, isn't it, Pedro?'

33

Pedro looked nervous as all eyes in the room were on him. 'Edward, my friend, you have made a mistake. I could never kill my Cherry, I loved her, even after she betrayed me.'

'No you didn't, and she didn't betray you. The affair never existed. It was all a work of fiction created by you and Gloria. Like pretty much everything we've seen from both for you over the last year or so, including your fictitious break-up.'

What?' Kimmy and Claire both said at once.

'They might be divorced on paper for the sake of their plot, but Pedro and Gloria never actually broke up, not in reality. It's all been planned the whole time, for Pedro to marry Cherry for her money.'

'But she was telling everyone who'd listen that he killed Frances,' Mum said.

'Yes, to keep us all convinced. Which was easy, because he didn't kill Frances, she did. While he had a genuine alibi with Claire at the B&B.' I noticed how shocked Claire looked. 'Poor Frances Flowers, she didn't even have to die for them to get their hands on Cherry's money.'

I looked over at Jacob, who hadn't taken his eyes off Gloria. I continued. 'It was important that Frances Flowers was found first, to keep the focus off Cherry's death and Pedro. If Cherry was the only death, or the first death, Pedro would have been under immediate suspicion. Obviously, Reverend Flowers would be the main suspect of his own wife's murder, especially after the affair revelation right before it.

'Which was another part of the plan, Pedro knowing full well that he'd already killed Cherry, but hiding her well enough that Frances would be found first. The snowstorm couldn't have been more perfect for their plan, and probably why they executed it when they did.'

So, everything we saw was fake?'

'Yes, Mum, everything. The accusation and attack of Reverend Flowers in the square, every public row you've seen Gloria and Pedro have, even the big, public, dramatic break up they had on Christmas Day. It was all carefully planned fiction.'

Kimmy looked in absolute disbelief. 'And you, Pedro, you pretended like you were being our friend in secret, behind Gloria's back.'

'They fooled everyone, Kimmy,' I said. 'Especially poor Cherry, who thought he'd fallen in love with her. He faked that love, even going as far as to marry her, which of course was to ensure he'd get her money. And his true love, Gloria, who he of course would have remarried afterwards, was in it with him the whole time.'

'I can't believe it,' Mum said. 'They both deserve Oscars.'

'I know, Mum. When you reminded me about their public break-up on Christmas Day, I remember thinking that it was a drama worthy of a soap opera Christmas episode. That's because it was. It was all carefully constructed drama.'

Pedro remained silent, but Gloria didn't. 'Listen, you little idiot. This is all rubbish, we don't have to listen to this, you've lost the plot.'

'I haven't, Gloria, and you know I haven't. I think the police will have an interesting time with your alibi now that Kimmy's has fallen through, not to mention the trainers and the phone records for both phones: the fake one and Frances' real one. But it wasn't just that, you and Pedro weren't as smart as you thought. You both gave me clues that you were involved.'

'I guarantee you that we didn't,' she replied arrogantly, before adding hastily, 'because we weren't involved, of course.'

'Part of the plan was that Pedro had married Cherry in secret, although only Kimmy and Claire knew that, and you definitely didn't. But when I spoke to you the second time and mentioned

Cherry as Pedro's wife, you didn't bat an eyelid. Because you already knew – it was part of your murderous plan.'

'You stupid woman!' Pedro shouted. 'All this trouble and you give yourself away like that!'

'Shut up, Pedro!' she shouted back. 'Who's giving us away now, you idiot!'

I smiled to myself – I had them. But I couldn't resist letting Pedro knew where he slipped up too. 'And you, Pedro, you said to me earlier that you *heard* I'd spoken to your ex-wife. I thought Claire or Kimmy must have rang you as soon as you left the B&B, but you came up with some story about seeing me with Gloria. Of course, the real reason you knew was because she'd warned you, because you were in on it together. Not to mention that you referred to her in the past tense, saying you *loved* her, and that she *was* beautiful, before we'd even found her body.'

Pedro stood up, and I saw a flash of the rage he'd shown Reverend Flowers this morning when he attacked him: although that was faked, whereas this was entirely real. 'You think you're so clever, don't you, my friend? You think you have worked everything out. Well, now you know what I am capable of, you better watch your back.'

'Alright, I think we've heard enough! Come on, Wood,' Appleby said as both men moved to grab Pedro, before Appleby read him his arrest rights.

'And where do you think you're going?' I heard behind me, as I turned to see Kimmy and Claire stood in front of the pub door, blocking it from Gloria, who was trying to exit during the commotion with Pedro.

'We need back-up... Gillespie, Bowie, Ortega, Underwood... come to the Chalk Inn now. We have suspects to apprehend,' Appleby spoke into his radio. Moments later, several officers descended on the pub as everyone looked on in amazement.

Mum stood by the door as the police led Gloria and Pedro out. 'Oh, Gloria, not that you'll be around for a while, but just so you know... you're barred.'

As Pedro passed us, Mum directed her last comment to me. 'See, I told you it's always the husband. I just had the wrong one.'

34

'Edward, that was amazing! You were incredible, you were just like Hercule Poirot. And what an ending to the mystery... the fake break-up solution, a rarely used trick in murder mysteries. I'm so glad you asked me here for a de-brief.'

I was in the church hall, formerly our incident room, and I'd asked Noah to meet me privately; I had a lot to discuss with him.

'Thanks, Noah, I thought you'd like it. I'm just glad we got justice for Cherry and the Flowers family. But I wanted to talk to you about a specific part of what I said in the pub. Do you remember when I said Everest Brown got Reverend Flowers' help to come find a member of his family? He actually came to look for his son.'

'Oh yes, I knew he was a red herring!' Noah said. 'I guess his son must be Jacob, which is why he went to Reverend Flowers. Did Mrs Flowers have him before she met the Reverend?'

This had actually been my first theory before I'd realised the truth. 'Not quite, Noah. The Reverend is Jacob's real father. But it is someone else very close to home.'

He thought for a moment, and as the seconds passed I could see him falling deeper in thought as he looked ahead, miles away. I didn't want to disturb him until he'd finished.

Finally, he spoke. 'It's me, isn't it? I'm the secret son he came to find. Well, that's alright if he is, I've never had a father before and he seems very nice. Is it me then?'

'Yes, Noah, it is. Everest Brown is your father.'

35

I'd put the pieces together after I realised Everest wasn't Jacob's father. I did think he was for a while, and even suspected him briefly as being involved in the murders, but I soon knew that he wasn't.

Mum was immediately worried they were going to lose their position fostering Noah, but Everest said he just wanted to get to know Noah; he wasn't here to take over, and I could tell he was a genuine man.

I'd brought Noah back to the pub and introduced them both properly, and they were now sitting at a table together with Noah chatting away to him happily. Everest nodded me at appreciation as I glanced over on my way to the bar.

'Edward, buddy.' I turned around at the bar to see that Patrick had followed me from our table. 'I wanted a quick word, just you and me. Well done for earlier, you were incredible. You blew us all away, it was fantastic.'

'Thank you,' I said, trying not to blush. I wasn't looking for glory, I was just glad that we'd got to the truth.

'The conversation about exes before though,' he said. 'That was really about Pedro and Gloria? You were checking your theory.'

'You got me,' I said. 'But I'm glad you're over Kat, I was actually worried for a moment there.'

'Look who I've brought home!' we turned to the pub door to see Appleby there, with PC Wood next to him. They both stepped aside to reveal Reverend Flowers.

'Dad!' Jacob shouted from his seat with Kimmy and Claire. He jumped up and ran to embrace his father. 'I'm sorry, Dad, I'm so sorry.'

'You have nothing to be sorry about, Jacob. I'm the one who's sorry. Your mother would be proud of you.' I looked away and gave them their private moment; I knew they'd have a lot to talk about later.

'We have to go, mate,' Appleby said as he and PC Wood came over to the bar. 'The snow's starting again and we don't want to get stranded in the village, you've given us a lot of paperwork to get through. I just wanted to say, you did it again, Edward. I'm proud of you, and really grateful.'

'Thank you, mate,' PC Wood echoed. 'I really enjoyed working with you.'

'Thanks, both of you,' I said as both men shook my hand. 'And Dean, well done. You did our village and the police force proud.'

'PC Wood, meet me outside in a sec, I just want a quick private word with Edward,' Appleby said to the junior officer, who waved me goodbye as he left the pub. Appleby then leaned over confidentially. 'He doesn't know it yet, but I'm recommending that he soon becomes DC Wood. I'm asking if he can join my team in CID.'

With a wink and a smile, Appleby too left the pub. Just when I thought all the thank yous were over, I heard a voice behind me.

'May God be with you, Edward.'

'Reverend, I'm pleased to see you.'

'Edward, I can never, ever repay you for what you did for my family. I hope my wife can rest at peace knowing you've brought justice for her. And may God forgive me for suspecting it was my son who killed her.'

I looked at the heartbroken face of the man in front of me. 'Reverend, you were manipulated and tricked by two very evil people who knew exactly what they were doing. And from what I saw a moment ago, you and your son will be fine.'

He smiled at me. 'Edward, I said a moment ago I can never repay you. I can't, but I do have a small gesture to make as a thank you, one that I know will prevent you from tremendous earache in the years to come.'

I was utterly confused as he called out to my

mum. 'Linda, I have something to ask you. You've probably realised that Pedro and Gloria's absence has created a couple of vacancies on my winter market. Would you like one of the spaces?'

'Oh bless you, Reverend!' Mum said, as she rushed to hug him.

Reverend Flowers simply gave a wink as he whispered to me. 'God bless you, Edward Crisp.'

EDWARD'S NEXT MYSTERY...

Kieron Juniper is one of the most promising young footballers in England. Quickly leading his football club, **Beachy Head United**, to incredible Premiership success, he has become a local and national hero.

But he has a secret. One that will make history. He is about to come out and become the first openly gay Premier League footballer.

Until he is murdered by someone who doesn't want that to happen.

Can **Edward** and **Noah** navigate a world of WAGs, drag queens and misbehaving millionaires to solve the **DEATH IN THE CLOSET**?

ACKNOWLEDGE-MENTS

I can't believe I'm here again. It seems like five minutes since I sat down to write the *Who Killed Miss Finch?* acknowledgments, when it's actually been nearly five months.

I want to thank every reader, reviewer, social media follower, friend and family member who has supported me since. Every second since release date has been a dream come true, I still can't quite believe it.

Again, I need to give a big thank you to Graeme, the most amazing partner anyone could ever wish for. You are my everything and I wouldn't be where I am without your support.

My family have always been there for me, but in publishing my book I've been reminded what a supportive bunch you are, even 300 miles away. Mum, Dad, Karen, Steven, Sarah, Harry, Harry, Alex, George, Alice and Ada, I love you all. Alice, you will be giving me a run for my money as an author in a few years! And Mum, you are the perfect proofreader.

Writing can often be a lonely occupation but I have an amazing team in place who have helped bring The Snow Day Murders to you.

To the fantastic husband and wife duo, Ben and Marion, for everything you do for me. Marion, you are such a talented designer and I'm so privileged to work with you: thank you for the beautiful cover. Ben, my 'go to' writer friend, always on hand to answer any manner of stupid questions about writing, advertising, Amazon, Facebook… everything! Thank you a million.

Charlie, thank you for your work helping name characters and being a sounding board for my ideas; I think you had a hand in pretty much every new character name this time round, and it really helped me bring them to life. DC Gillespie will eventually get more to do, I promise!

Harry, our housemate, thank you for being a brilliant first pair of eyes and for all your feedback, suggestions and errors spotted. PC Wood is for you!

Jon, my amazing ad designer, I have never seen such a combination of kindness and talent, and I know everyone at Bowden House agrees!

The Grove Theatre - Steve, Dave and Ori - for all of your support in hosting my book launch and lending your premises to record my audiobook (Ori, you are a legend), and being all round great guys.

To Kate and the team at Old Town Community Library, Eastbourne, thank you and I look forward to being able to do something in person really soon.

Juliette and Nigel at Heathcliff House, thank you for your support; Kimmy and Claire might be both women but there is a little of you two in their lovely B&B and homemade jams!

To one of my lovely readers, Chris George, thank you for the info about farmers' help in previous local snowstorms. Very useful and I hope you like the farmer's name!

My ARC team for all of your support in reading in advance and for all the kind words / reviews, with a special shout-out to the fabulous Bookstagrammers Phil, Hannah, Zoe, Lisa and Michelle for being incredible Instagram cheerleaders!

My dear friends, in Wigan, Manchester and Eastbourne - North and South, old and new - I love you all. Especially the ones who read a book for the first time in years to support me!

And to all the other writers I've met along the way; it's so lovely to have such great people on the same journey as me.

Thanks again to all of you: love you all and I hope you all remain safe and well in these challenging times. See you all for book 3!

KEEP IN TOUCH!

Thank you for making it to the end of Edward's latest mystery; I hope you had as much fun reading as I did writing it! Did you figure out *The Snow Day Murders*?

I love to hear from readers, so if you have any feedback, spotted any errors you wanted to tell me about, or just wanted to say hello, you can reach me at peter@peterboonauthor.com.

Alternatively, do come say hi at my social media pages:

Facebook.com/Peterboonauthor
Instagram.com/Peterboonauthor.

Finally, the best way to help an author is to leave a review of the book, so if you have a spare moment, I'd love it if you could leave a quick review on Amazon.

Thanks again, and see you next time to see if you can solve the *Death in the Closet*!

Made in the USA
Middletown, DE
15 August 2022

71445517R00139